DEDICATION

For Gene L. Coon

June 7, 1924—July 8, 1973

"Gene celebrated life. With honesty, candor, love, generosity, humor—yet he delighted in insisting he was a hard-nosed s.o.b. . . . He was an authentic war hero. . . . Yet he was very much against war and killing. So he built an armor around his gentle heart, of toughness and humor. . . . Any way you looked at Gene, you saw a loving man. He loved his family. . . . He loved people. He loved reading. He loved writing with a joy I've never seen in another writer. . . . Gene had a literary streak, and so I've adapted an old Latin verse by the poet Catullus, just for him, for now:

> *By ways unknown and many mem'ries sped,*
> *Brother, to this moment am I come*
> *That I may celebrate the dead*
> *And speak of peace with your ashes dumb.*
> *Accept my thoughts. Such heirlooms of past years*
> *Are joyous things to grace you where you dwell.*
> *Take them, all drenched with a brother's tears.*
> *And, Gene, my brother, now, hail . . . and farewell."*

(Excerpted from eulogy by
John J. Furia, Jr., President
Writers Guild of America)

The People in Questor's Life

JERRY ROBINSON
A brilliant young engineer who must re-learn the meaning of the word "friend-ship."

EMIL VASLOVIK
The aging scientist whose mysterious disappearance threatens Questor's ex-istence.

DR. GEOFFREY B. DARRO
Head of "Project Questor," he sets out to destroy the android he helped build.

LADY HELENA ALEXANDRE TRIMBLE
Whose beauty was matched only by her wisdom and generosity.

1

Jerry Robinson felt no more for the object lying on the instrument assembly pallet than he felt for any other computer assembly he had constructed in the past seven years. The fact that this computer had the shape of a male human being in every particular had little bearing on the work he did. He glanced up from a monitoring device to look at the object for which an entire top-security lab had been built.

It had an average build—about five feet eleven inches and not overly muscular. Still, heavy metal straps held the arms and legs in a spread-eagle position on the assembly pallet. Jerry could not think of it as anything other than *it*—the android Emil Vaslovik had left for a five-nation science combine to build. But the thick metal restraints had been insisted upon by Michaels, the British scientist.

"It resembles an ordinary human body," he had said. "But there is a tempered steel framework under that plastiskin and an energy source to give it power beyond all human capacity. If anything goes wrong in the lab, I want to be assured it won't break loose."

So Michaels had been assured, and the android had been strapped down. Jerry saw no menace in the android. Perhaps he had worked on its component parts too long. To him it appeared to be only a man-shaped thing with sleek, hairless skin and no details at all to make it seem human. The bald head had basic nose and ear shapes in the proper places, but the mouth was only a slit—lipless. The eyes had been inserted, and the thin plastiskin eyelids were closed; but there were no brows or lashes. The body had no nipples or navel. Nowhere were there any of the

1

blemishes, scars, wrinkles, or other tiny flaws that human bodies carry.

Jerry thought ruefully of the long scar on his left shin, the result of a childhood bicycle accident. It could be covered, if he had enough vanity about it to go to a plastic surgeon and go through the skin grafts. *One up for the android,* he thought. Any scars it acquired could be neatly repaired in a matter of minutes with a heat molder.

Michaels' voice broke in on his thoughts. "Ready to disconnect?"

Jerry stepped closer to the android's side and scanned the contact points of the control and readout wires that led from the exposed circuitry to a telemetry unit overhead. The flap of plastiskin had been pulled back at the right side of the abdomen, laying open the intricate and astonishingly small servo-units, electronic relays, and microscopic transistors that would, supposedly, bring the android to life. There was doubt, in some quarters, that the project would succeed. Most of the android's components had been designed by Emil Vaslovik before he inexplicably vanished three years ago, and not one of the scientists or technicians in the room could explain what half of them were or how they worked. Or were supposed to work. The acid test would come in a few moments.

Satisfied that the contacts had been doing their job, Jerry nodded to Dr. Michaels. "Ready to disconnect, sir."

"Disconnect it from the lab controls."

Jerry began to remove the leads, his deft fingers moving with the skill of one whose craft is both instinctive and well learned. A bluish pulsating glow came from a power unit deep inside the android. The color intensified as Jerry removed the fine wires one by one.

The scientists and technicians hovered over control and monitoring devices as the young microelectronics engineer worked. Their ID tags identified several as Nobel Prize winners in their fields. The white "clean suits" gave them all a uniform, bulky look, except for Phyllis Bradley, whose spectacularly contoured figure could not have been defeated by an old-fashioned diver's suit. She was also one of the Nobel Prize winners.

Jerry completed the disconnections and stepped back a pace. Suddenly the android's chest heaved; Jerry caught his breath, startled. The rise and fall of the machine's chest steadied into a regular pattern, and Jerry became aware of the voices routinely reporting.

"Heartbeat simulation steady at eighty." This from Michaels.

Phyllis Bradley flicked her gaze across a console and nodded in satisfaction. "Respiration simulation holding at twenty-one. Epidermal reading, 98.6. Internal lubricant flow, normal; full circulation. Pulse registering normal."

Jerry moved to the android's side again. It lay unmoving except for the rhythmic rise and fall of the chest in a normal breathing pattern. The eyes remained shut. The flawless skin and lipless mouth made it seem suddenly alien and disquieting. Jerry tentatively reached out to touch the android. The plastiskin was warm, but far too smooth. He had almost expected a human reaction—perhaps a ticklish drawing away. There was none, of course; he pulled back his hand, vaguely uncomfortable.

"It's doing nicely on its own." Michaels looked up in time to see Jerry withdraw his hand, and he frowned. "Have you met a problem there, Robinson?"

"No, sir. When its chest started moving, it startled me, that's all."

Gorlov, the Russian, shook his head. "Strange you should be alarmed. This great toy of ours—you were most prominent in constructing it. You knew what it should do."

"Maybe I didn't really believe it would work."

Gorlov appeared surprised but had no chance to comment. Geoffrey B. Darro entered the security lab. He was dressed like the others, in a white clean suit, wearing the obligatory identification tag and radiation-level badge. Jerry always knew when Darro was around, even if he hadn't seen him come in. Everyone instinctively fell silent and waited to be spoken to.

Darro was a man few people questioned. If they did, they seldom received answers. There probably was a dossier on him—somewhere—but most of what was known about him was only what Darro himself cared to reveal. Physically, he was a rugged, broad-shouldered man, still showing the easy, fluid motions of a well-conditioned athlete. He might have been fifty—there was a little gray in his crisp, dark hair. Intellectually, he was an accomplished man with a broad grasp of history, politics, economics, international strategies, and interplay on all levels. He was fluent in five languages and unyielding in all of them. Personally, he seemed to have no friends, no associates, no soft spots or weaknesses. At times Jerry was sure that Darro was made of harder steel than the android.

Darro was the official head of the five-nation Project Questor primarily because he was the one individual on whom they could all agree. He had been hired by many nations in the past—sometimes to overthrow a government, other times to save one. He never broke his word or his contract, and any country which employed him never regretted it. Geoffrey B. Darro's integrity was as dependable as the rising and setting of the sun.

Darro's eyes flicked around the room, taking it in with one look. The others went back to their monitoring rather self-consciously. The project chief crossed to the cosmetology section, where Dr. Chen was using a computer screen on which color slides flashed up. The finely detailed pictures were followed by complete information on the molding of features, skin pigmentation, hair implantation, and on other cosmetic instructions.

"Decided on the features you'll give it, Doctor?"

Chen looked around at the big man standing behind him. "Naturally, I would prefer Asian, Mr. Darro. I see great beauty in the shape and color of my people's faces." He smiled ruefully. "But when we hooked up its eye units, they turned a rather occidental blue."

Darro grunted. "Apparently Vaslovik had his own ideas on what he wanted."

"One of his many reputations," Chen said. He turned to the computer and keyed in a new diagram.

The screen obediently displayed a large color schematic of the mechanism which served as the android's eyes. The rounded front surface resembled an anatomical rendering of a healthy human eye. Chen tapped it with a finger.

"The part of it we will see looks remarkably human and will probably have normal eye movements, secretions, and so on."

Chen pushed another switch, and the diagram changed to reveal the complex microelectronic structure behind the rounded front area. Chen shook his head. "But exactly how the eye mechanism *operates* is still guesswork." He switched the screen diagram again, bringing in a closer, more detailed view of the delicate works. "We have never seen half the microunits Vaslovik used here. Or in the other components, for that matter."

"Fully disconnected," Robinson said from behind them.

Darro turned and moved back toward the assembly pallet. Dr. Bradley scanned the body monitor again. The levels were all satisfactory and no different from any average-human-body readings, as far as they went. There was no brain activity, no muscular movement except for that required by the rise and fall of the chest and the pumping of lubricant through the veins. "Readings excellent. Running very smoothly on its own," she said.

Michaels nodded and gestured to Jerry. "Seal it up, Mr. Robinson."

Jerry picked up a heat-molding tool and triggered it. The tip glowed red in a few seconds. He moved the flap of plastiskin into place, covering the exposed transistor packs in its side. The android's chest continued to move in even cadence, and Jerry hesitated for an instant. The eyes were closed, and the head still looked alien. *It's a machine,* Jerry reminded himself. *Get on with it.*

He applied the molding tip to the loose flap, holding the plastiskin in place to assure smooth bonding. The "skin" sizzled, but the accompanying odor was not unpleasant. Some smoke curled up from under the molding tip as Jerry moved it along the flap.

"You're not burning it?" Darro asked.

"No. That's just normal residue in sealing up." Jerry stepped back so that Darro could see. The sealed area was clean and smooth, totally unblemished, as if the flap had never existed.

Darro nodded, impressed. "Another of Vaslovik's little inventions?"

"Mine." Jerry shrugged lightly. "I knew we'd need something like it. If it's supposed to look like a man, the seams can't show."

The project chief studied him intently but did not comment. Jerry had a feeling that the fact was registered, filed, and could be recalled instantly if Darro needed it. The young engineer turned his attention to the android.

Dr. Audret moved an information-input device over the android's head. It was a dome-shaped object, linked directly into the lab's programming computers. Audret glanced over at Gorlov. The Russian activated the data-tape turntables. Jerry shifted his weight nervously, impatiently, and Darro instantly snapped his attention from the android to the engineer.

"Programming ready," Gorlov said.

Darro watched Jerry. "The moment of truth."

Jerry suddenly stepped forward, his hand instinctively reaching out in a plea. "Please! I'm sorry—but I think you're wrong to use your programming instead of Dr. Vaslovik's."

The scientists turned to look at him with some surprise. Dr. Audret was the first to speak. "Monsieur Robinson, I think we all consider you a talented young engineer, but since this *is* a scientific decision—"

Jerry interrupted, turning to Darro as project chief. "Mr. Darro. Dr. Vaslovik's notes *specifically state* we should activate it with *his* programming tape. They now want to use their own computerized, hybrid mush—"

Darro cut in, hard and cold. "As project administrator, Mr. Robinson, I will not interfere with scientific decisions. Nor will you."

"It is a useless discussion," Audret said. "We all know half the Vaslovik tape has been erased—"

"By the attempts of *your* cryptographers to decode it," Jerry snapped.

Gorlov muscled into the debate, interposing himself between Robinson and Audret. "Naturally we wished to learn what instructions Dr. Vaslovik left for the android. Unfortunately, we did not."

"No, you only managed to destroy what might mean the success of this project."

The Russian lifted his hands in a little gesture of acknowledgment. "Once we saw there was nothing to be gained and only certain loss if we continued, we ceased to experiment with the Vaslovik tape. We have selected university tapes of your systematized knowledge since our tests show that orderly data fed into the android will form patterns in the brain-case bionic plasma."

Darro glanced back to Jerry. The young engineer was upset. To Darro, he seemed more concerned than a technician should be over the proposed programming.

"How can you be that sure?" Robinson demanded. "All we've done is assemble the parts and material Vaslovik provided, and no one here even understands them or—"

Darro interrupted him again, the hard edge still in his voice. "No more than I understand this change in the normally cooperative Mr. Robinson. Is it possible, when you worked for Dr. Vaslovik, that you learned something you haven't told us about?"

"I didn't even know what he was training me *for*. He never so much as mentioned an android."

"Then you have no valid argument against the step proposed by the scientists, have you?" Darro looked around at them again and nodded. "Enough debate, gentlemen. Please proceed."

Gorlov and Audret moved away to the computer controls and activated them. The reels of programmed information began to spin . . . first one, then another, until four of the dozen began to register, status lights flashing on the consoles. A flicker of colored-light pinpoints reflected from the information-input dome down onto the android's smooth, bald skull.

Jerry nervously bit his lip, his eyes darting from computers to android and back. Darro watched Robinson. But, like the others, even the implacable project chief ultimately was drawn to the unmoving figure on the assembly slab.

Phyllis Bradley bent over the EEG oscilloscope, hoping to see something but afraid she would not. There were so many unknowns . . . Suddenly the straight line on the scope fluttered and then began to pick up a muted pattern. She kept her voice impassive, fighting the surge of excitement she felt. "Getting brain-wave readings."

Jerry stepped forward slightly, unaware of Darro's scrutiny. He *had* seen a movement in the android. The thumb of the right hand twitched. *There* . . . it jumped again! There was a moment of nonmovement. Jerry had a fleeting impression that the only creature in the lab that had moved was the android. Everyone else was suspended in mid-breath, waiting. Then there was a slight, convulsive twitch of the right leg . . . again . . . and again.

Gorlov, practical and pragmatic as always, turned to Darro. "This run includes mathematics, engineering, various sciences. Although we cannot expect the android to understand or use such information, it will begin setting orderly patterns."

"The greater the number of these molecular patterns, the more likely it is that it will be capable of simple thought processes," Audret said.

The computer data tapes spun to a halt, and the soft accompanying hum ceased. Everyone's eyes went to the android. But the man-shaped thing lay still and unmoving again.

Dr. Bradley's voice whispered across the silence. "Brain-wave production, zero."

"Well," Michaels said briskly, "only a first try. We have a good deal more programming to feed in." He motioned to Gorlov and Audret, who busied themselves with the other computers.

Again, the reels began to spin, the hum growing louder as the full ensemble of twelve gradually engaged. The flickering pinpoints of light bombarded the android's skull in a dazzling dance of color. The exact method of information absorption was not understood—another of

Vaslovik's inventions. The android's limbs quivered slightly, much less than before.

Darro had not missed the difference in response. "Dr. Gorlov?"

Gorlov tried to sound hopeful. "The limited results of the first run indicate that many more patterns will be necessary." He glanced pointedly at Robinson. "We *are* using Dr. Vaslovik's specified input procedures."

"This run is longer," Audret said, "giving far more patterns, far more complex than the initial ones. University tapes on logic, literature, medicine . . ."

"Let's hope you haven't burned it out," Jerry said.

He nodded toward the android. It lay immobile, with the single exception of the breathing motion of the chest. The tapes on the twelve computers spun to a stop, and Phyllis Bradley consulted the EEG oscilloscope.

"Cerebral activation, zero. No brain waves at all this time."

Jerry examined the toes of his clean suit with intense interest. Darro almost wished the engineer would say "I told you so" just to get it out of the way. Jerry chose to let it hang there, implied, in the disappointed silence that clogged the atmosphere of the lab.

Audret finally spoke. "We have no option but to try the Vaslovik tape."

Darro flicked a look at the small computer, which stood apart from the others. Its size and shape differentiated it from the prim, square mechanisms that crowded together in the computer section. The tape loaded on its reels was also a sharp departure from the norm in color and width; and when Gorlov activated the machine, the tape whirled at a different rate of speed. The polka of varicolored light pinpoints began to play over the android's head.

For a moment, nothing happened. Then, abruptly, the android's body went into convulsions. Jerry jumped back as the torso and limbs strained against the heavy metal straps. The thing's arms and legs flailed at the restraints with superhuman strength; but the face remained expressionless, the eyes still closed. The voices of the science-team members bubbled up, drowning out the hiss of the turning tape and the clatter of the android's limbs against the assembly pallet.

The tape ended, and the android's body fell back on the slab, limp. Jerry Robinson had held more hope for Vaslovik's programming than he cared to admit. The failure of the android assured a failure of Jerry's faith.

2

The Cal Tech lab was littered with all the data that had been applied to Project Questor from the beginning, three years before, to the moment of failure on the assembly slab. The scientists conducted a postmortem that went on for six hours. Jerry Robinson sat with them but did not contribute. He was rummaging around in his own thoughts, trying to avoid the shards of shattered hopes. Darro stood slightly away from the group, watching and listening, weighing the arguments and reactions.

Gorlov's voice rose stridently over the others. "It is *impossible* to overload its brain case. Dr. Vaslovik's own notes indicate a billion billion potential configurations."

The android lay on the assembly slab, all but forgotten in the debate over its construction and programming. The basic activation devices still functioned, also forgotten.

"It should work!" Bradley said. "Every stage of assembly tested out perfectly."

The android's eyes snapped open, a bright, pleasant blue, clearly conscious and menacing without brows or lashes to soften them. It turned its head toward the conference table where the science-team members sat. The overhead lights in the assembly area had been turned off, and the android's slight, noiseless move went unnoticed.

"Perhaps some basic error made by Vaslovik?" Chen suggested. "On a project such as this, one might become so subjective that some slight miscalculation would be easy to overlook."

"Not likely," Jerry said. "Not Vaslovik."

Michaels nodded and pushed a pad around on the

table. "I agree. Every unit Dr. Vaslovik provided worked as predicted."

"Unless he built in some factor his notes do not mention. I agree with Dr. Bradley . . . it should work!"

Darro finally stepped forward. He moved deliberately, assuring their attention before he spoke. "I think we're all quite naturally disappointed. May I suggest a fresh start tomorrow?" He held up a hand to wave off the rumble of protests that began immediately. "We've all had a long day, and you've pored over the project notes for hours. You need some time off to gain a fresh perspective."

"I expect Monsieur Darro is correct." Audret stood and gathered up some of the papers. "But I intend to study these further in my quarters."

As the other scientists rose, the android snapped its head back to its original position and its eyes closed. Jerry walked to the banks of still-glowing equipment and began to turn off various controls.

Darro watched him without appearing to be studying his every movement. Was the engineer just doing his job, or was he dallying behind in the hope of being left alone with the android? Jerry completed shutdown of the computer complex. He was turning to the EEG oscilloscope when Darro's tap on his shoulder stopped him.

"Leaving, Mr. Robinson?"

"Yes, right away," Jerry said. He flicked off the oscilloscope and the main medical monitor. "No need to waste all that power on a failed project." Darro followed him through the lab and out into the changing room. As he went out, Jerry turned off the main laboratory lights, leaving on only a few work lights here and there to illuminate the big room.

In the silent lab the android lay on the assembly pallet like a figure cut from stone. But on the pen-needle track of the Brain Wave Log, the stylus jerked and trembled, inscribing the android's brain activity on graph paper—belying the stillness of the body.

Darro delayed until all the scientists and Robinson had left the building. Then he approached the security guard seated at the desk in the entrance alcove. The guard had been glancing impatiently at his watch, looking for his relief; but he snapped alert when Darro stopped beside the desk.

"Evening, sir."

Darro grunted something that sounded like a response. His eyes scanned the check-out list bearing the signatures of every person who had entered and left the building each day. All personnel except for the guards and himself were accounted for.

"I want this entire building under full security tonight. Tell your relief I'm calling in two extra men. They'll identify themselves by name and badge number. Check it against the master security list."

The guard frowned nervously. "Yes, sir. Anything wrong?"

"No. And I want to keep it that way." Darro glanced along the narrow hallway that led toward the changing room and security lab. Abruptly, he turned and started back to the lab. A second security guard, patrolling the corridor, joined him.

The changing room was deserted. A few lockers still stood open, the white edges of discarded clean suits poking out like ghostly fingers. No one would enter here until six-thirty the next morning, when the first shift maintenance crew came in. New clean suits would be brought in at seven o'clock, before the project team arrived. No one was allowed in the locker room or lab at night.

Darro checked the inner security door, then the television monitor, which was trained on the still form of the android. He tapped a zoom button and the image drew nearer. The body seemed the same as before. Darro studied the screen, then turned to the laboratory door.

The locks were in order, as Jerry had closed them. Darro opened them systematically and entered the lab. The security man remained at the door. Darro was not the kind of man who looked over his shoulder on dark streets, but something about the dimly lighted room bothered him. His eyes swept the lab, seeking whatever it was that had suddenly alerted his senses.

Nothing was out of place. Nothing added nor taken away. The air-conditioning and humidity control hummed gently. A few control lights glowed. Everything seemed normal, but Darro felt something out of order.

Moving quickly, he crossed to the assembly pallet and examined the android. It looked as it had before the attempt at activation. He touched it. The plastiskin felt smooth and cool, definitely below body temperature. He hesitated for a moment more, then examined the metal restraints on the wrists and ankles. Everything was as it should be, except that Darro still felt that something was wrong.

He finally turned away and joined the guard at the door. "I want this area closed off all night. No one is to come near it, got that?"

"Yes, sir."

Darro pushed shut the door and engaged the locks. He could see into the lab, and it still looked normal. Pushing aside the apprehension niggling at his mind, he firmly turned his back on the locked door and left.

The sound of Darro's footsteps going in one direction and the guard's in another registered on the android's sensitive hearing apparatus. As soon as the two humans had gone, its eyes snapped open and looked down at the thick metal straps that bound it to the assembly pallet. It briefly evaluated the situation, then tensed its muscles and lifted its arms. The restraints broke with a scream of outraged metal. The android sat up and examined the ankle straps. Since there seemed to be no difference between these and the wrist restraints, the android simply reached down and pulled them loose as easily as if they had been made of soft wax.

It sat on the pallet, its eyes and ears taking in and cataloging the laboratory in detail. The preliminary scan accomplished, it looked down at itself and recalled the things it had to do. It brought its body temperature up to the required 98.6 and activated the internal mechanisms that produced pulse, heartbeats, and a normal respiratory action. Jerry Robinson would have been surprised to learn that the android could control these activities without the

aid of the expensive equipment that crammed the laboratory.

The android carefully maneuvered itself to the edge of
the pallet, swung its feet down to the floor, and stood. It
swayed, then quickly made the necessary internal balance
adjustments. Its back was very straight, and as it took its
first step, it registered the fact that this stiff posture was
not correct. It loosened the body muscles slightly, flexed
the knee and ankle joints, cataloged how much balance
control came from the toes. Another step revealed how
weight must be shifted, how arm motion also helped
stabilization. The android absorbed, filed, and used information in a fraction of a second. As soon as the problem of walking was sufficiently mastered, the android
moved to the computer banks and began to activate them.
Its movements were purposeful, planned, and ominous.

3

Geoffrey Darro's office was as straightforward as he was. The room was large and decorated in attractively cool colors. No clutter, no piles of paper, comfortable but clean-lined furniture, files with discreet but stout locks. One file folder lay open on the table Darro used as a desk. The neatly typed strip on the tab read ROBINSON, JEROME BAKER. Darro flipped past the usual ID photos and fingerprints to the sheaf of background data. His administrative assistant, Walter Phillips, entered quietly and set a stack of teletype sheets at Darro's elbow. He waited until the project chief looked up.

"Robinson's academic records. I've just discovered that large eastern universities do not like having to dig out alumni information after closing hours."

"But they did it."

"You have friends at M.I.T."

Darro turned back to Robinson's file. "I want a personality profile on him. Try Washington. Wake up whomever you have to."

Phillips nodded and left, knowing that Darro had friends in Washington, too. Perhaps more important, Darro knew that Phillips would carry out the order, and the information would be in his hands as fast as it could humanly be obtained.

Jerry Robinson appreciated complex machines, which may have been one reason why he could never get vending machines to work properly, if at all. The coffee machine in the project living quarters was the only dispenser available at that late hour, and he was forced to face it. The

16

machine accepted his quarter and waited for the selection. He punched the button for cream—no sugar, and the machine coughed out a paper cup but no coffee. Jerry hit the side of the machine, but nothing more happened. He hit it again, with the same result. Just as he was turning away, the dispenser maliciously began to spurt gouts of cream and a trickle of coffee. Jerry took the paper cup with the acceptance of a confirmed vending-machine victim.

"Ah, Mr. Robinson, what a fortuitous meeting. I was hoping to find you."

Jerry turned to look into the smiling face of Dr. Chen. "Good evening, Doctor." He waved to indicate the vending machine. "Coffee?"

"Thank you, no. Are you returning to your room? I'm going that way."

Jerry shrugged. "Sure. Come along." He absently took a sip from the cup and grimaced down at the light beige cream. Then he realized what Chen was saying.

"I would like to discuss a certain proposition with you . . . one which I believe you would find quite profitable."

"Dr. Chen, I don't know any more about the project than you do," Jerry snapped coldly. "I'm simply following the blueprints which you and your colleagues have thoroughly studied."

"Of course, of course. But on the other hand, you did work for Dr. Vaslovik."

"In the same way you work for your government. I followed orders—which is exactly what I'm doing now."

Chen moved closer, clearly not believing Jerry. His voice dropped confidentially. "But Vaslovik insisted that *you* be retained for the assemblage. Really, Mr. Robinson . . ."

"Look, I've said it before. I'll say it again. I know how to install servo-mechanisms and diodes and triodes and tetrodes—but I don't know *why* in this particular assembly."

"Someone else has talked to you—"

Jerry interrupted brusquely, "Dr. Chen—get off my

back." He shouldered the smaller man aside and strode away toward his quarters.

The small suite of rooms assigned to Jerry, as to each member of the project team, had become a home for him in the past few years. He was used to it and found it comfortable. The bed-sitting room was cheerfully decorated in colors of the occupant's selection. Jerry had chosen warm yellows and browns, with splashes of orange. The adjoining room was a workroom, where Jerry had set up his drafting board and shelves for books. At twenty-nine, he had not acquired many material possessions except for those items directly concerned with his work. But several pen-and-ink sketches and watercolors of his own were included in the art on his walls, and the compact stereo tape deck was one he had designed and built himself. The selection of tapes ranged from the classics to the music of Dylan and Kristofferson. The bars on the windows were the only things he hated about the building.

Jerry felt the key turn a little too easily in the lock, but he had stepped inside before the fact fully registered. Phyllis Bradley and another American stood facing him. He noticed that the man had smoked two cigarettes and stubbed them out in the decorative ashtray on the end table beside the soft leather couch.

"This is my room. What are you doing here?"

"Mr. Smith and I just want to talk to you, Jerry."

"Smith!" Jerry snorted. "What kind of alphabet soup are you? FBI? CIA? ONI?"

"Sit down, Robinson," Smith said.

Jerry stared at the man, sat down, and stared again. Smith. The name was as nondescript as his appearance—exactly what was required in his kind of work. He was a pale man, gray eyes and blond hair as washed out as an old dish towel. Jerry did not miss the fact that the suit, which seemed a bit oversized, neatly hid a heavily muscled body and the ever-so-slight bulge of an automatic.

"You are an American citizen, Robinson. If you are working under secret instructions left by this Vaslovik—if you are withholding information—or if you have made a personal agreement with one of the participating powers . . ."

Jerry tiredly interrupted, "Who do you think I sold out to?"

Phyllis Bradley took a step toward him, troubled by Smith's line of attack. "Jerry, that thing in there—the country that controls its manufacture could control the world."

"As I understand it, that is exactly why Vaslovik insisted it be a joint project of the five powers."

"Then think of your own country, Robinson." Smith had softened his approach, and Jerry decided that he liked him better the other way. "If that robot in there finally functions—"

"*Android*," Jerry said. "Not a robot. And it would be functioning already if Dr. Bradley's pals hadn't been so suspicious of Vaslovik—and each other—that they wound up erasing half the activating tape."

Phyllis looked away from Jerry's accusing stare. "That was a mistake. We admitted it."

"Robinson, if that—android—falls into the hands of an unfriendly power and they duplicate it thousands of times, the rest of the world would virtually be helpless."

Jerry stood up impatiently, shaking his head at Smith's persistence. "If, if, if. The android can't be duplicated. The entire supply of bionic plasma Vaslovik left has been installed in the android's cranium. Take any of it away, and it won't function at all."

"Anything can be analyzed and reconstructed," Dr. Bradley said.

"Really?" Jerry said acidly. "You people tried to for six months and failed."

"Where is Vaslovik?"

"I wish to God I knew."

Suddenly the door to the corridor opened, and Geoffrey Darro stepped in. Smith started to move for the automatic, then his hand stopped and went back to his side, limply. There was an armed security guard standing behind Darro.

"Both of you, get out of here!"

"I'm not sure you have that authority, Mr. Darro," Smith said.

"On this project I have any authority I choose to exercise. Read my contract."

"Robinson is an American citizen."

"Exactly," Darro said. "And he is under contract to a supranational scientific authority. Read *his* contract." He flicked a look at Phyllis. "And, Dr. Bradley, report to the conference room. There's a meeting in five minutes."

"I thought we'd had a long, hard day."

"Doctor, half an hour ago I learned that the French and the Russians both were planning to abduct Mr. Robinson and the android. They feel someone is double-crossing everyone else. Since Robinson is the lead technician and an American, they decided the double-crosser was you. And they may have something there."

Phyllis turned on him angrily. "That's possible, but I have another nominee. You saw the test run. The mechanism should function, but it doesn't. *I* think it was Vaslovik, working through his protégé here."

"I wasn't his protégé! I was one of fifty technicians working on his various projects."

"Be that as it may," Darro said quickly, "from now on, no one speaks to Mr. Robinson privately, except for me."

Smith raised his eyebrows suspiciously. "How do we know we can trust you?"

"You take my word for it." Darro met Smith's stare and glared him down. "Now get out of here. Oh . . . and if you decide to come visiting again, you'll find the security guard posted at Mr. Robinson's door."

Smith and Dr. Bradley left silently. Jerry glanced after them, then back to Darro. "I'm not sure I like that," he said. "The guard, I mean."

"Like it or not, Mr. Robinson," Darro said, "he stays."

The android sat before the mirror in the cosmetology section, studying its own smooth, hairless face and body. The table bore an array of dyes, creams, special heat-molding tools. An image flashed briefly in its brain—a picture of what it should look like. Then the image was gone. Gaps . . . too many gaps in information. Program lacking.

The cosmetology computer keyboard was at the left. The android turned to it and activated it. A schematic came on as the screen glowed to life. The android studied it, keyed in a new instruction. Then, faster and faster, it began to go through the entire cosmetology computer bank, until the individual schematics became a blur.

The computer completed the run and stopped. The android was motionless for the space of a minute, analyzing and correlating the information it had absorbed. Then its eyes flicked down to the table, and it picked up a heat-molding tool. It examined the tool briefly and found the activating switch. The android reached down again and located the already cast mouth mold. It fitted the special device onto the basic heat unit and turned the cosmetology mirror toward its face.

This second look at itself, with its new information, triggered a new response. The android blinked its eyelids for the first time. Finding the effect satisfactory, the android activated a program of eyelid movement that corresponded to a natural human pattern.

Then it opened a jar of reddish pigment, applied a thin coating to the interior of the mouth mold, and switched on the tool. When the tool was ready, the android carefully raised it to its lipless mouth and pressed the mold into place. It sizzled, and smoke curled up from the hot mold as it met the plastiskin. The android's face remained expressionless, except for the regularly blinking eyelids. It removed the mold, revealing human lips, perfectly natural in shape and color. The android tilted its head slightly to the side, studying the final result. Then it reached for the ear mold.

The conference room in the project quarters was sound-proofed and regularly checked by security guards for wire-tap and monitoring devices. Yet the room was intimate enough to encourage a free flow of discussion at the round table that dominated. The five scientists and Darro were seated around the table. Darro's assistant, Phillips, occupied a chair in one corner of the room, unobtrusively taking notes.

"For the moment, I will table the matter of the conflict of interests various members of this team have indulged in. You are here to make the android operational. I have reason to believe this is not possible," Darro said.

A chorus of startled exclamations rose and fell around the table. Darro hushed them with a brief wave of his hand. "That does not imply a failure on your part."

Gorlov leaned forward. The room light bouncing off his glasses made his eyes appear as two sheets of silver foil. "Are you suggesting that someone is preventing the android from functioning?"

"I've been troubled by a number of puzzles since I came to this project, Doctor. For example, as scientists, just how do you assess the parts of the android you do understand?"

"We've all agreed it is a remarkable outpouring of new discoveries and inventions, to say the least."

Darro noticed that Phyllis Bradley had not looked at him or the others when she spoke. "Too many for one scientist, Dr. Bradley?" he asked.

She did not raise her eyes. "Vaslovik's genius is well known—Nobel Prizes for his work both in nuclear fusion and in biotics, for example."

"But if you ask, would a *group* of scientists be more believable . . ." Audret paused, considering it. Then he nodded. "I think, yes."

"We have discussed this among ourselves, of course," Gorlov said. Heads bobbed agreement around the table. "Vaslovik has always been something of a mystery to the scientific community."

Darro pushed back in his chair and rose. "Vaslovik—disappeared or presumed dead. Or is he?" He paced restlessly, almost thinking aloud to himself. "Did he drop out of sight voluntarily? Why was this project left to this five-nation combine? To guarantee that all nations would benefit from it? Or to get the brains and resources necessary to get it constructed? Perhaps for other uses." He turned back to them as a ripple of agitation went around the table.

Dr. Michaels was frowning, puzzled. "But you do not think we can activate the android. Obviously, you are wondering if Mr. Robinson fits into your premise."

"Very much so," Darro said. "I've learned from his university records that our pleasant, unassuming micro-engineer has a tested intelligence quotient fifteen points higher than any person in this room."

The android completed the implantation of eyebrows. It had done the delicate installation of lashes in a tenth of the time it would have taken Chen. The eyebrows required even less time. The android paused again and regarded its image in the large mirror. Perfectly formed ears had been molded from the rough shapes that had adorned the bald head. The nose had been sculpted into a less-than-perfect line. Whoever had designed its features had decided that the android would not look like a Greek god.

The plastiskin had been treated to produce texture, wrinkles, a mole here and there, even a small fan of lines at the corners of the eyes. Nipples, navel, toenails, and fingernails had been added, along with a small scar under the chin and another on the inner left calf.

The android consulted the material on the cosmetology table and found the coarse blond hair to be implanted in its head. There was another instrument to stitch the sections of hair into the scalp. The android lifted the first section of hair, carefully positioned it, and started the implantation mechanism. As the stitches drilled into the bald scalp, the android followed the progress reflected in the mirror, automatically adjusting for the reversal of the image. All the facial adornments had been added, but the android's expression had not changed. It was immobile, blank. The lines in it had been impressed into it, not earned. The eyes glittered hard and cold—and inhuman.

Jerry Robinson flicked a look at his watch, surprised, when someone knocked at his door. It was eleven, long past the hour when anyone came to the project building. Even internal visits tapered off around ten because of the rigorous work schedule Darro had established. Jerry opened the door to find the project chief standing there.

"Evening, Robinson."

Jerry nodded, waiting. Darro raised an eyebrow and stared a hole through him. Jerry stepped back a pace and vaguely gestured inside. "Uh . . . come in . . . again." Darro moved past him, and Jerry closed the door. "Little late, isn't it?"

Darro settled himself comfortably in an overstuffed chair. "Your usual routine is to retire at eleven-thirty. Since you're alone and not working, I assume I'm not interrupting anything."

"Is there a monitor in this room?"

Darro twitched the corners of his mouth in what passed for a smile. "Not at all. Your habits are regular and seldom vary. Even if the project members *were* monitored—and they are not—your personal life runs along as dependably as a clock."

"I didn't think I was that dull," Jerry said thoughtfully. "But you didn't drop in to tell me people can set their watches by me."

Darro nodded briefly. "Quite right. I've just come from meeting with the project scientists. After reviewing all of our information and options, we've decided that the most practical use of the android will come only if we disassemble it."

"Disassemble it? But . . . you *can't* order that!"

Jerry was aware Darro watched him critically, but he couldn't contain the surprise, the anguish that burst from him. There was too much of his life bound up in the building of the android. The successful completion of the Questor Project was as important to him as breathing. He tried a new tack. "You pulled those scientists off me only two hours ago. Now you're saying you've approved the destruction of the entire project."

"I pulled them off you, as you put it, because I will not have that kind of double dealing in any operation I head.

Disassembling the android does not destroy the project, Robinson. The participating nations will still get a rich return on their investment, won't they? Its so-called stomach, for example—a nuclear furnace that was believed impossible. But it works, and I represent five nations that are very anxious to take it apart and find out *how* it works. And other parts of it, too . . . turbine pumps the size of match heads, electrical circuitry using gas vapor—"

Jerry interrupted desperately, "But a *functioning* android, Darro. It could change the shape of this whole world! The space program, undersea exploration. It could change industry, agriculture . . ."

"An excellent summary of its socioeconomic implications, Robinson. Especially from a man who calls himself 'simply a gifted mechanic.' "

"That's what I am."

Darro pushed out of the chair quickly, impatiently. "We have a full dossier on you. Every IQ test you've taken since you were in high school indicates the same thing—genius-level intelligence."

Jerry sat down automatically, staring at Darro. The project chief turned away from him and opened the window. The action seemed meaningless until Jerry realized that Darro was studying the ornate grillwork on the window—the bars of his prison. "Hey, look . . ." Jerry started.

"That *is* true, isn't it? Or are you labeling all those tests a lie?"

The young engineer relaxed in the chair and found a laugh. *"Me,* a genius? Sorry. Darro, that was just a fluke. I do well on IQ tests because I'm a puzzle solver." He tapped his head. "Some twist up here gets a kick out of intricate things."

"Like androids which should work, but don't."

"You sound like you think someone's going to the lab tonight, push some button on it and say, 'Follow me.' " He shook his head, chuckling at the ridiculous image. Darro slammed the window, and Jerry's smile faded when Darro turned, his face grim and set.

"Not entirely impossible, Mr. Robinson. Is it?"

"Even if it was, why would I want it?" Jerry got to his feet angrily, pushing in at the unmoving project chief. "To play chess with? To hold for ransom? Follow me *where?*"

"Perhaps to a man who has been presumed dead even though a body has never been found."

Jerry stared at him, his mouth open. Finally he managed to pull himself together from the shock of the suggestion. "Vaslovik?"

"He may have found a five-nation combine an attractive idea. Ample funds and the world's top scientists doing the job his own organization couldn't complete."

"His organization? Darro, Vaslovik was a scientist of the highest caliber—but his 'organization' consisted of about fifty people who built from his designs. Research and development was done by him . . . only him."

"My point exactly," Darro said. "You don't know where he is?"

"Darro, if *you* don't, I certainly don't."

The project chief studied Jerry, the hard blue eyes cutting him into little sections and examining each one. Finally he twitched his mouth in that odd half smile. "You're one of two things, Robinson—either a remarkably shrewd, able man acting a part, or a very foolish man who doesn't recognize his own potential." He stepped to the door and opened it. Jerry could see the armed security guard still standing there. "Mr. Robinson is not to have visitors or leave his quarters except at my orders."

"Yes, sir." The guard did not question the change in Jerry's status. No one questioned Darro.

Darro glanced back at Jerry. "Good night, Mr. Robinson."

Jerry nodded weakly and watched Darro leave the room. The security guard reached in and pulled the door closed. The lock clicked from outside. Jerry slumped into a chair, head in his hands, wondering exactly what had happened. He was under guard and under suspicion of being some kind of saboteur, or at least potentially one. If only Vaslovik were alive. If only the android had functioned. . . .

4

The android, Questor, had opened every locker in the changing room. He had been built to resemble an average-size man, but his search for clothing had revealed the singular scarcity of average-size men in the group of scientists and technicians. He had disregarded underwear, not comprehending any need for it. A technician's striped sport shirt was tucked into a beltless pair of old chinos Dr. Chen sometimes wore. Dr. Michaels' locker had yielded a tweed jacket. Questor had found a pair of white socks stuffed into tennis shoes. The sneakers did not fit, but a pair of black shoes from another locker did. Sufficiently garbed, Questor stepped to a mirror. He tilted his head slightly to the right, surveying the image reflected in the glass.

He saw what appeared to be a blond, blue-eyed, fair-complexioned man in his thirties. The face that had been designed for him was attractive, but with enough flaws to be interesting. The clothing fit well enough. He saw no need for a tie and no incongruity in the white wool socks and black shoes. He turned away.

A red light gleamed beside the emergency exit to the security lab. The door was not normally used, but was linked into the alarm system. Questor studied it briefly, then reached out and pressed the glowing red plate. The light went off. The door did not open, and Questor turned his attention to it. The only projection was the doorknob. Questor pulled at it, and the knob came away in his hand. He bent to examine the hole left in the door, using his infrared capability to scan the dark interior. He understood his mistake then and would not make it again.

Questor straightened and scanned the door frame. A steel molding ran around it, preventing the insertion of anything between the frame and the door. Questor reached up, his fingertips carefully gripping the edge of the molding, and pulled it away from the wall. Effortlessly, his expression as untroubled as a statue's, he stripped the molding from the entire door. Then he slipped his fingers in the half-inch clearance on top and yanked the door from the frame. He neatly set it aside, and left.

The side door was a thick, heavy metal fire-and-security panel with a stout locking bolt. Questor paused as he heard the footsteps of the patrolling guard outside. As soon as the guard was well past, Questor bent aside the thick locking bolt and eased open the door.

His hearing mechanism amplified the guard's footsteps as the man walked along the front of the building. Questor set off across the grass at an oblique angle, reaching the sidewalk a slight distance from the lab. He noticed the difference in texture as he stepped from the grass to the cement, and paused for a moment to catalog the information. Then he set off in a direction that would take him past the front of the Project Questor laboratory.

The guard posted at the entrance looked at him without curiosity. Questor strode along ramrod straight, but with enough ease to draw a courteous nod from the guard. Questor logged the motion in a split second and nodded back. The guard seemed satisfied and looked away.

Questor angled off the sidewalk as soon as he was out of sight of the laboratory. He stopped under a stand of trees to get his bearings, and became aware of the soft undercurrent of night noises. A cricket chirped, a car purred along one of the dormitory driveways in the distance, the wind gently fluttered leaves overhead. Questor amplified his hearing and picked up the low murmur of two voices, a man's and a woman's. His eyes automatically tracked to the source.

A pair of students strolled along a walk some distance from him. They had their arms around each other, and Questor could hear the girl's low laugh. "What'll they say if they find me in your room?"

"We can say we're studying."

"They won't believe that."

"Why do we have to say anything?"

"You *always* have to say something."

The conversation meant nothing to Questor. He turned away, scanning the campus for the building he wanted, and located it two blocks away. He moved away from the tall trees and found his path blocked by a flower bed. Night-blooming jasmine scented the air, and he traced the fragrance to the flowers. His fingers stroked the delicate blossoms lightly, and he cataloged them.

As he walked around the wide flower bed and emerged on the lawn again, something made him look up. It was one of those rare, marvelously clear nights in southern California, and the whole glittering panorama of stars was laid out across the sky. Questor stood for a long moment, staring up, his eyes sweeping from quadrant to quadrant, studying them all. For the first time a trace of expression moved his face—the faint knitting of his brows, as if something puzzled him. Something he could not catalog. It was not the location of the stars. Their positions as seen from every point on earth had been programmed into him. It was something else, something undefined that had not been programmed but was a part of him anyway.

A rustling in the shrubbery behind him swiftly drew his attention back to his immediate surroundings. A large black and tan animal confronted him, ears laid back, a low growl rumbling in its throat. Questor tilted his head slightly to the right, trying to classify it. Part of his programming was jumbled and contained gaps. This was one of them.

"Good ev-e-ning," Questor said. His voice was flat, expressionless, the words disjointed.

The Doberman stopped growling and backed up a pace, confused by the android's strange voice. His nose quivered slightly and he took another step back, beginning to whine.

"Good ev-e-ning," Questor said again.

The Doberman spun around and sprinted away, his dark form disappearing in the shadows. Questor pulled

his brows together again. A most curious response. Surely
he had said the properly courteous thing. However, there
were important matters he had to attend to immediately.
He turned his attention from the animal.

Cal Tech was a stately campus, set like a jewel against
the Sierra Madres. Its older buildings had the graceful
architecture of a gentler, less frantic world. One of these
was the administration building. Questor mounted the
short set of stairs to the front doors and stepped into the
marbled corridor. A massive set of double doors faced him.
A sign beside them identified them as the entrance to the
Vaslovik Archives.

Questor crossed to the doors, took both doorknobs in his
hands, and twisted carefully. There was resistance, so he
twisted harder. The locking mechanism shattered with a
metallic scream; Questor entered, leaving the doors slightly
ajar behind him.

The Vaslovik Archives were sheltered in one large room
crammed with shelves of bound papers and locked filing
cabinets. There was also a microtape reading setup. All
the material stored in the archives had to do with Project
Questor exclusively.

There was no light in the room, but Questor needed
none. A slight adjustment of the eye mechanism, done
automatically, enabled him to switch to infrared. He went
first to the microtape reader. The machine was easy to
operate and would provide the most information quickly.

At the far end of the hall, a light shone in a single
office. A shadow moved against the opaque glass of the
upper door, and then the light went out. Allison Sample
emerged, locked the door, and walked quickly toward the
main entrance.

When she reached the Vaslovik Archives she noticed the
slightly open doors, and frowned. The custodians who
tended this building had never been careless enough to
leave that room open. She went to shut it, then heard the
sound of papers fluttering in the darkened room. She
glanced around quickly. There was no one else in the
building at this hour. If she went for the campus police,

the trespasser might make off with valuable material. But sometimes, she told herself, a bluff worked. She squared her shoulders, pushed open the doors, and snapped on the lights.

Questor looked up at the ceiling fixtures, and his eyes instantly adjusted to the new lighting. He had completed his study of the microtapes and bound papers, and now was busy with the files. The faint sound of someone breathing at a rapid rate shifted his attention to the door where Allison stood, her hand still on the light switch.

Questor studied her curiously. She was tall and slender. Questor automatically calculated her exact height and weight. Her short dark hair framed a fresh and completely open face. The impression of honesty was bolstered by the wide, intelligent blue eyes staring back at him. She was twenty-eight, competent, completely trustworthy—as proven by her top security clearance—and had been Vaslovik's secretary and administrative assistant. In fact, she still handled all the project paperwork and maintained the archives.

"Good . . . evening," Questor said. His voice was still flat and expressionless, but he had smoothed out the individual syllables, so the greeting sounded a little more normal.

"What are you doing here?"

Questor tilted his head to the right, quickly absorbing the nuances of Allison's low voice. "Vocal inflection. Yes . . . interesting."

Allison felt tension draining away from her. If the intruder meant robbery, surely he would have bolted by now. Yet this pleasant-looking man with the peculiar speech pattern merely stood at the open file, a folder in his hand, studying her.

"I asked, what are you doing here? Who are you?"

Questor began to scan the folder again. But his vocal inflection had improved, giving a touch more naturalness to his extremely formal word selection. "To the first question, I am scanning various minutiae in search of required data input."

Allison said softly, "Oh."

Questor glanced up at her, noting her raised eyebrows, her expression of puzzled surprise. Obviously facial features, as well as voice inflection, altered as mood and incident required. He would have to practice that. As he returned to his scan of the file papers, he said, "As to the second question . . . I am part of Project Questor."

Allison frowned thoughtfully. "I've never seen you around that building."

"Around?" He was lost for a second, as the word failed to compute in the contexts he knew. Then data slid into place, and he recognized the reference. "As a colloquial phrase, meaning 'in the vicinity.' "

Allison eyed him nervously, but her curiosity was piqued and she was determined to get an explanation. "Who *are* you?" she asked again.

Questor finished scanning the file in his hand, replaced it, and dug out another. "If this is to be an information exchange, then the next interrogative is logically mine. Who are you?"

"I'm Allison Sample."

Questor paused and looked up. "Allison Sample is Professor Vaslovik's media intermediary."

"Uh . . . yes, his secretary." She smiled for the first time. "That helps. A complete outsider wouldn't know that."

Questor took note of the smile and flexed his facial muscles in an imitative response. It wasn't a very good smile, but it apparently was done well enough to convince Allison while he tangled with another colloquialism. "Outsider . . . to mean a stranger, a possible threat." He went back to flipping through the file. "To relieve apprehension, I can supply other information, Miss Sample. Jerry Robinson is the assembly engineer on Project Questor. He was employed by Vaslovik four years ago to—"

Allison interrupted eagerly, "Do you know Jerry well?"

Questor pondered the question, then replied honestly. "He has been closer to me than any other human."

"I like him, too," Allison confided. "Say, where are you from? It's a most unusual accent."

"It is my speech pattern. I must make it more colloquial. How much do you know of the Questor Project, madam?"

Allison's eyebrows lifted again. "I prefer 'Miss Sample.' But I really must know what you're doing here. These archives are not generally open."

"There is little I do not know about the project . . . Miss Sample."

"You make me sound a million years old."

"That does not seem entirely logical, since you obviously—"

"You know you sound like Professor Vaslovik?"

He ignored the half question. "Project Questor has reached a stage that absolutely requires that Professor Vaslovik be located. If you can be of any help . . . ?"

Allison shook her head, troubled. "I only know he seemed to be quite ill . . . then he disappeared, leaving behind this five-nation arrangement to carry on the project."

Questor sensed that she was upset and concerned for the missing scientist. The emotion was something he could catalog but could not understand. He changed the subject, more to gain information than to calm her. "Was he known to enjoy aquatic vehicles? I have a . . . fragment of memory associating him with such a thing."

"If by aquatic vehicles you mean boats, no. You *are* the strangest man."

He replaced the last of the files and looked at Allison again. "I have spent most of my life in the laboratory, thus I no doubt lack social graces."

Allison ducked her head, hiding a smile. She could not know that Questor would not understand why she found his flat statement so amusing. "It . . . does show a little, to be perfectly honest."

"This concerns me," Questor said, "since I am about to leave on a journey which may require them."

He brushed past her and through the open doors into the marbled corridor. She followed, startled by his abrupt exit. A small sound of protest started in her throat and died as he stopped and turned back again.

"Farewell, madam." He paused, realizing something more should follow. "Parting is such sweet sorrow."

Allison stared at him, unable to summon a syllable to cover her surprise. Then she found herself smiling at him, charmed and amused by his solemn, terribly formal manner. "I do hope you're going with someone on this trip?"

"Yes," Questor said somberly. "I see it is quite necessary. Thank you."

He moved again to leave, and she involuntarily reached out after him. "You do have a name, don't you?"

Questor stopped, half turned to her, and hesitated. He searched his mind for an answer and found the only one that fit. "Yes, Miss Sample. My name is . . . Questor."

He left as quickly and quietly as he had come. Allison made no move to stop him. She was paralyzed by the impact of what he had said. *Questor? There is no one on the project named Questor. There is only—the project.*

5

Jerry Robinson had gone to bed after Darro left. He had suddenly felt weary, and not only because it had been a long day. He had been more disappointed than he wanted to admit when the android failed to function. The following conferences, overtures, and accusations had added to his worries; so he took refuge in sleep. Now he dreamed, again and again seeing the android as it strove for life on the assembly pallet—and failed.

The shadow that darkened the grilled window did not disturb him. Subconsciously he heard the faint, reverberating *bing* of metal being bent aside, and thought it was part of his dream. The gentle sound of the window being raised did not disturb him either. He had reached the part of his dream where the android thrashed and strained against the bonds on the assembly pallet. Suddenly, strong fingers clamped across his mouth and nose.

Jerry's eyes flew open, and he sat up, panicked. The light from the window revealed only a male figure bending over him. The man spoke quietly, in a curiously flat, expressionless voice.

"Mr. Robinson, I mean you no harm. I must speak with you."

Jerry stared up at the stranger and nodded. He had no other choice: he was almost smothering. The man promptly removed his hand and Jerry took a deep gulp of air. When his breathing steadied a little, he demanded, "Who are you?"

"I am Questor."

Jerry looked up again, puzzled for a moment. The stranger moved aside slightly, and Jerry caught sight of the iron grillwork that had been wrenched away. Then it sank in. There was only one . . . thing . . . that could have bent those bars so radically and so silently. The stranger —*it*—regarded him calmly. Jerry tried to make a break for the door, but Questor's arm shot out and firmly held him where he was.

"Please do not call out, Mr. Robinson," Questor said reasonably. "I am programmed to prevent that if necessary."

Jerry subsided, again, having no choice. He knew that the android could break his arm twice as easily as it had bent the grillwork. Jerry had *built* the thing, after all. He tried to think, organize a plan, but all he could see was this creature standing over him—a creature that looked, simply, like a man in his early thirties. The hair, the brows, the skin texture, had all been done with great finesse. Studying the android now, Jerry realized that it must have followed the cosmetology instructions to the last detail. He should have recognized Questor immediately, but he had been accustomed to thinking of it as the smooth, hairless piece of machinery he had constructed.

That was it.

"If you know my name, you must understand. I am the human who put you together."

"I do understand that."

Jerry scrambled off the bed and backed away from Questor. His voice shook slightly as the android followed him step for step. "You *must* obey my instructions. You hear me? I am ordering you to—"

The door lock clicked abruptly and the guard came in, machine gun in hand. "I thought I heard . . ." His eyes swept the scene: the warped grillwork bars, the stranger confronting an apparently intimidated Robinson. He started to turn the gun on the intruder.

Questor moved faster. He recognized the guard and the gun as dangers as soon as the door opened. He grabbed the barrel of the machine gun with his left hand and squeezed. At the same second, with his right hand he touched a spot just behind the man's ear. The guard collapsed like a deflated balloon.

Jerry bent over the man as Questor quietly closed the door. He was relieved to find that the guard was only unconscious. The pulse and heartbeat were strong. Jerry looked up as Questor spoke in that curious monotone.

"My university tape programming was most helpful, Mr. Robinson." He gestured toward the guard. "The human anatomy information allowed me to select a nerve which will keep him unconscious for approximately one hour."

"Naturally you don't have that vulnerability," Jerry said shakily.

"You are well aware of that, Mr. Robinson. As you pointed out, you constructed me."

Jerry pulled himself together and controlled his voice. "Right. And, as I also pointed out, you have to obey me. *I am ordering you to return to the laboratory!*"

"I am grateful for your advice, but I must leave immediately for a metropolitan complex known as London." His hand descended to Jerry's shoulder. "And it is essential that you accompany me."

Jerry felt the tremendous strength of the android's fingers pressed into his shoulder, though Questor was obviously careful not to hurt him. But all he could do was stare at the machine gun, which had fallen beside the guard. The barrel was flattened and bent into a right angle. And the hand resting on his shoulder had done it.

6

Jerry Robinson drove the freeway's slowest lane, heading west on the Golden State, merging into the Ventura Freeway, maintaining a speed of fifty. The android seated beside him attentively studied the night-lighted scenery, the traffic flow, the ramp signs, but he did not question Jerry's operation of the car. Possibly Questor had not absorbed the principles of driving. Jerry's mind raced over alternatives and plans for escape, but he kept running into barriers. He knew he might be able to engineer a minor accident that would disable the car. But that involved physical risk to himself and possibly to innocent bystanders. Besides, the android's reflexes were faster than his and he could probably prevent it. He knew Questor was quicker and stronger than he was. Trying to escape on foot would be useless, and combat ridiculous. All he could do for the moment was go the slowest, longest route possible to Los Angeles International Airport and try to dissuade the android with logic. He cleared his throat, and Questor turned his head to look at him.

"You realize this is insane. Don't you understand you belong back at the lab? There is so much work to be done yet."

"The work has been done."

"You're not capable of making that decision!" Jerry fought down an impulse to keep on shouting. Logic. Calm logic was the only answer. "Look . . . you know I literally put you together. I installed your—your brain. I fed in the program tapes."

"I am quite aware of that, Mr. Robinson. I have intended to ask you why your programming was so incomplete in one area and so redundant in another."

Jerry wriggled his shoulders uncomfortably, and his friendly face twisted into a scowl. "That wasn't my idea. The scientists tried to decipher the Vaslovik tape, but all they did was destroy—" He switched suddenly to indignation, annoyed at himself for forgetting what Questor was. "I don't have to answer questions from you. You are supposed to do what I tell you. Respect and obedience . . . respect and obedience."

"But I do respect you, Mr. Robinson, and I shall cooperate in all logical ways. Why are you not prepared to do the same in return?"

"Because you are a machine!"

A car cut into the lane ahead, just missing Jerry's front fender. He braked and snarled an obscene comment about the driver's birth and misbegotten lineage. Then, remembering, he glanced over at Questor. The android watched him quietly, apparently unfazed by the near miss.

"Cogito, ergo sum," Questor said.

"What?"

"A rather important philosophical aphorism, first enunciated by the French philosopher Descartes."

Jerry nodded and automatically guided the car into the cloverleaf ramp that would take them onto the San Diego Freeway heading south. "I think, therefore I am. What makes you think you think?"

"Quite perceptive, Mr. Robinson. That question has been troubling me as well. *Cogito, ergo sum. Am I?"*

Jerry kicked himself mentally, realizing what he had done. He could have continued on the Ventura Freeway, not turned south onto the very road past the airport! Maybe, if he was careful, he could ease onto the Santa Monica or Long Beach Freeway, both of which crossed this one. That would divert them long enough . . . long enough . . . for what?

"Am I?" Questor asked again.

"Just thinking doesn't mean you're alive," Jerry said distractedly.

"Since I function—crudely at times, I admit, but I feel I shall improve, with your help—your statement does not seem totally relevant."

"If you're so damned perfect, why do you need me?"

Now it was Questor's turn to pause and think about his reply. He frowned slightly, but Jerry was too busy driving to notice it. "Because," Questor said slowly, "my instructions are incomplete."

"You are simply an *ambulatory computer device*. Do you accept that much?"

"Completely."

Jerry allowed himself a small sigh. "Good. Now, as a human being with years of experience in this human world, I'm telling you *we can't go to London*."

This time he saw Questor tilt his head slightly to the right. It was an inquisitive, puzzled gesture, and very human. Where had the android gotten that?

"I have no choice but to try, Mr. Robinson. My creator's programming tape included that I go to him. As quickly as possible."

"Do you know that he's in London?"

"No."

"Do you know if he's even alive?"

"No. Yet I cannot disregard that command. I must find him. London is a beginning."

"That tape was damaged, partially erased! So whatever instructions Vaslovik left you could be garbled, twisted . . ."

"Incorrect," Questor said patiently. "The imperative to find Vaslovik was perfectly clear. It is his location which was erased and fragmented. Do human minds contain such specific imperatives—or are they all as random and disorganized as yours seem to be?"

Jerry snapped his head around toward Questor. "Listen, it was a human mind which conceived of you . . . humans who put you together . . ."

"Please attend to the operation of the vehicle, Mr. Robinson."

Jerry looked back at the freeway in time to avoid running up the rear of a big double rig. Questor's voice went on levelly. "I have no desire to appear hypocritical, but I find it astonishing that precise and voluminous knowledge of the various sciences helps so little in the understanding of human behavior."

"We get along."

"I am not entirely convinced of that," Questor said.

"This is ridiculous. *I will not argue with a machine.*" Jerry leaned back in the seat, fuming, clenching the wheel with white-knuckled hands. Then he noticed the image of the police car in his rear-view mirror. It was a California Highway Patrol black-and-white, routinely patrolling. Jerry casually slid his left hand off the wheel and turned off the headlights.

"Resume nocturnal illumination, please."

Jerry winced and reluctantly turned on the lights. Questor turned to study the other cars moving around them. "It seems only logical that we emulate the practices of the other vehicles."

"Right," Jerry said wearily. He saw the police car going off the last exit ramp they passed. No help there. "Do you trust me?"

"Yes," Questor said promptly.

"Good. This is not the way to the airport."

"Incorrect. We are now precisely 11.24 miles from the air-vehicle terminal. This roadway will deliver us to a lesser artery leading directly to the terminal complex."

"There's no possible way you can know that," Jerry snapped incredulously.

"I glanced at a metropolitan diagram in the Vaslovik Archives."

"You took *one* look at the city map?"

Questor nodded calmly. "You installed my vision components quite well, Mr. Robinson. It is because of my flaws in other areas that I vitally need your assistance. More than my creator's location was erased from his tape. I seem to have no . . . explanation of myself. Can you inform me why I must find my creator?"

Jerry frowned and held the wheel tighter. "I'm beginning to worry about that, too. A lot."

The guard had come to precisely an hour after Questor had dropped him. It took him ten minutes to get to Darro's room, wake the project chief, and explain. Five minutes after that, Darro was dressed and standing in Jerry's quarters, surveying the damage. The guard sheepishly rubbed his neck, still embarrassed. Darro's assistant, Walter Phillips, picked up the machine gun and handed it to his boss. As he did, he tapped the impossibly flattened and bent barrel.

". . . then I heard voices," the guard was saying. "One was Mr. Robinson saying something about it having to obey his orders."

Darro examined the smashed machine gun. "Describe the android's appearance, please," he said impassively.

The guard shrugged. "Well . . . just a guy. Average. But when I went in, I never saw anything move so fast."

Phillips had moved over to the window and touched the bent grillwork bars. "Mr. Darro, if it should get out there's something like that loose which can do this . . ." he touched the bars again, then looked back at the weapon, "and that . . ."

"I see no reason to risk a panic by identifying it. I'm not even sure anyone would believe it. Robinson obviously controls it very well." He turned abruptly to the security guard. "Have my full staff assembled in my office in five minutes." He waited until the guard left before he spoke to Phillips. "The android is functional, as far as we can tell. It must have a certain amount of mental facility, and it clearly has full physical capacity."

"Do you really think Robinson controls it?"

Darro considered it, then shook his head doubtfully. "It's possible, but who can say? The android broke out of the lab by itself and came here. The guard said Robinson seemed to be afraid of the thing. But he didn't get too good a look before it put him out."

"Painlessly," Phillips pointed out. "He didn't hurt the man."

"I might point out that that could have been sheer accident." Darro gestured toward the door with the ruined machine gun. "We've got work to do."

Traffic into Los Angeles International Airport was always heavy, even late on a weekday night. The roar of the jets landing and taking off was almost constant, nerve-tearing if one stood outside too long. It was past midnight, but all the terminals were alive with people departing and arriving. The vast parking areas in the center section were almost full. Jerry pulled his car into a lot opposite the long terminal building housing the international carriers and managed to slide into a space another car had just left.

He sighed, feeling as if he had already completed a wearying journey. Almost as an afterthought, he switched off the ignition and lights. Then he turned to Questor and studied him intently for a long moment. The android silently stared back, waiting for him.

Jerry nodded with ironic satisfaction. "I'll say this much for you. It's an engineer's dream to have something this complex come together so perfectly. I almost wish I could go with you to London, study how you react to different situations."

"But you are accompanying me to London, Mr. Robinson."

"Will you try to understand that that's impossible!" Jerry snapped. Then he stopped, gathered in his flaring temper, and tried to be logical. He had to remember logic with this thing. "There are many reasons why not. For example, it would require six to seven hundred dollars for us to purchase travel to London." He dug into his jacket pocket and pulled out his wallet. Opening it, he thumbed through the money and showed it to Questor. "And I have a total of . . . thirty-three dollars."

The android took the wallet and examined it for himself. Jerry smiled triumphantly as Questor said, "I understand. Contemporary economic practices were included in my university tape programming."

Jerry began to feel a warm glow starting. At last! He had gotten through that peculiarly stubborn programmed response and the android could see *his* logic. "Good. We're finally beginning to communicate. You see, there's a difference between things we'd *like* to do and things we *can* do."

Questor had completed his rapid examination of the wallet's contents and sat listening carefully. He looked up at Jerry and nodded. "Thank you. I comprehend perfectly."

"*Good.* And flying to London is something we can't do."

"Incorrect, Mr. Robinson. Since Vaslovik's records on you included your economic reputation, I was certain we could travel to London using one of your delayed-specie cards." He lifted several credit cards from the wallet and held them out.

Jerry stared at him, stunned. The android displayed the cards for him as innocently as a child. He *was* innocent in many ways, but Jerry had suddenly had it. Rage churned up in him, shaking his body and his voice. "*You* are planning to use *my* credit cards?"

Questor nodded calmly. "Is it not a quite common way of . . . ?"

Jerry grabbed the wallet and cards out of his hands and stuffed them back into his jacket pocket. "*I have had it! With Darro . . . with you. Jerry Robinson is finished being pushed around by humans or machines!*" He slapped his hand on the car-door handle. "Now, I'm going to open this door and leave. You can knock me unconscious, but keep in mind that you can't get on an airplane carrying me. From now on, you're on your own!"

He opened the car door; but as he started to get out, Questor's arm shot across his chest. He was pressed gently but firmly back into his seat. Questor's face remained blank as Jerry glared at him. *Why couldn't he understand what went on behind those expressionless eyes?*

"My imperative will not allow me to release you, Mr. Robinson. Your subsequent actions could prevent me from finding my creator."

"What are you going to do then? Kill me?"

"Thank you," Questor said flatly. "That is the logical alternative."

Jerry felt his heartbeat thundering at a reckless speed, but he remained still, staring steadily at Questor. The android stared back. Then Questor dropped his arm.

"Strange. I find it impossible. I must endeavor to continue alone."

Jerry promptly got out, slamming the car door after him. He hunched his shoulders against the damp, chilly air that always seemed to hang over the airport at night, stuffed his hands into his pockets, and started to walk away. He took five steps before he hesitated, took another, then stopped. This should be easy. Why couldn't he just walk away? Darro would find the android, even if it got as far as London, which he doubted it could. But something made him go back to the open car window where Questor sat, unmoving.

Jerry leaned in. "Look, I can almost understand what's driving you. We humans . . . we spend a lot of our lives sort of seeking our creator, too. But you can't abduct people, commit immoral acts in doing it."

The android looked at him innocently. "Humans do not commit immoral actions in seeking their creator?"

Jerry looked away, shaken by the question. How could anyone answer that—honestly? He decided it was safer to divert the android for now and try to figure out a reply later. "Look, *you can't make it alone!* You'll give yourself away, there'll be panic, probably bullets. You're too valuable to be damaged or destroyed. And innocent people could be hurt."

"Then it seems most logical to me that you come with me, protect me, guide me in areas of morality. I will accede to any request which does not violate my programmed imperative."

"I'd like to believe that," Jerry sighed.

"You forget I am merely an ambulatory computer device, Mr. Robinson. I would find any deception quite difficult."

Jerry shot a suspicious look at Questor as the android evenly repeated that he was merely an ambulatory computer device. Was he? He was capable of so much more than even Jerry thought he had been programmed for. Could he lie, too? Was he lying now? Questor returned Jerry's look with his now-familiar calm innocence. Only after they were actually on the plane and airborne did Jerry realize that he had stopped thinking of Questor as "it" and had begun to regard him as a man.

Lydia Parker brought a tray of discarded glasses and empty miniature liquor bottles back to the galley in the waist of the 747. Her fellow stewardess in coach, Jean Klein, glanced around at her as she began to stow the plastic glasses. "Getting along all right?"

Lydia smiled. "So far, my first transatlantic flight is a cinch."

"Night flights usually are. Light load, and most of the passengers try to sleep."

Lydia nodded and straightened up. "I've got two who look like they're playing owl. One of them's reading everything onboard."

Jean peeked around the galley entrance. "Which?"

"Fifty-nine A and B. Can you see them?"

The long rows of high-backed seats prevented a good view, but Jean could make out the two men seated alone on the port side of the big cruiser. "Maybe they can't sleep."

"Well, they certainly do *read*."

Jerry had watched Questor whip through a thick pile of newspapers and magazines. The android read a sheet in a glance, tearing through the publications as fast as pages could be turned. Jerry found that he had suddenly developed a habit of jumping nervously whenever anyone approached. In the meantime, Questor carried on a conversation as he read, apparently at ease doing both.

"Do you know if Vaslovik had any affinity for aquatic vehicles, Mr. Robinson? I was able to ascertain that he did not own one."

"Sailing, yachting, that kind of thing?"

"I believe so. A fragment from my creator's tape seems to associate his location with such a vehicle."

Jerry puzzled over it, trying to remember his casual conversations with the scientist. Vaslovik seldom discussed outside interests. Jerry had had an impression that Vaslovik had very few, at least none he had taked about. "I don't recall Professor Vaslovik ever mentioning any boat or ship. Look, I'm more interested right now in something called *passports*. In London, they'll discover they weren't packed in our luggage." His voice dropped to a desperate whisper. "We don't even *have* luggage!"

"I have a plan," Questor said calmly. "My programming included detailed information on international law and procedure."

Jerry stared at him, startled. "That *wasn't* part of the university programming."

"I referred to my creator's tape. It is puzzling why he would consider this necessary. Also, my compulsion to acquire information on your world. It must be satisfying to be human and know the reason for one's existence."

Fleetingly, Jerry wondered if Questor was teasing him, but decided he couldn't be. Nothing the android had said even hinted at a sense of humor. Questor was absolutely serious, of course. "Maybe we're not so different," Jerry said. "Not in that way, at least."

"At least you know you are alive, part of a world of living things. In my case . . ." Questor paused, bemused. "Strange, I almost stated that I *feel* loneliness. Is it possible I was meant to feel and that this was among the things erased from my creator's tape?" He resumed reading.

Jerry studied him for a long moment before he answered. "I've no way of knowing what he did intend for you. I'm sorry, Questor."

The android's bright blue eyes came up and rested on him. The head tilted slightly to the right, quizzically. " 'Questor.' The first time you have spoken to me by name, Mr. Robinson. Thank you." He dropped his attention back to the magazine.

"Slower," Jerry hissed suddenly. "No one can read that fast!"

Jean Klein came down the aisle with a fresh stack of magazines, wanting to get a closer look at them. Questor reduced his reading speed, but it was equal to riffling the pages. Jerry jammed an elbow into Questor's ribs, and he looked up to see the stewardess staring at him, bewildered. Questor carefully turned a page and concentrated on it. Jerry gave the young woman his brightest, most charming smile. She relaxed, smiled back, and put down the new stack of material.

"My, we do read a lot, don't we?" she said conversationally.

Questor looked up, eager to open a new subject. "I am delighted we share that predilection, madam. However, I find printed information most inefficient compared to computer data readout when used—"

Jerry interrupted, handing the stewardess the pile of discarded publications. "Miss, could I have a martini, please? As large as regulations permit." He flashed his most dazzling smile again.

Jean decided she had been right. They were both nervous fliers, trying to cover it. She nodded pleasantly to Jerry and turned to Questor. "And you, sir?"

Questor had resumed his reading. "No, madam. Although I am capable of simulating imbibing and ingesting, there seems little reason at this time to—"

"My friend doesn't want a drink, miss. That's what he means."

Questor recognized the desperate warning tone in Jerry's voice and glanced at the stewardess. She looked puzzled and on the verge of asking embarrassing questions. He understood instantly and nodded his agreement with Jerry's interpretation. "I do not wish a drink."

Jean studied them both for a second longer. "Are you feeling all right, sir?" she asked Questor.

He had gone back to reading. "Functioning perfectly, thank you."

She nodded skeptically and left. Jerry breathed a sigh of relief and reflected that this was getting to be a habit, too. "Questor . . . until you get the hang of things, why don't you let me do the talking?"

"I thought I performed quite well. Was the form of address correct?"

"Yes, but—"

"Were sentence structure and grammar correct?"

"Well . . . yes. Formal, but—"

"Then we are 'in,' as you would say."

In defeat, Jerry slouched down in his seat and folded his arms. "*I* wouldn't say that."

Darro's office at Cal Tech had been transformed into a communications center. When Phillips walked in, he was reminded of the battle operations station of the aircraft carrier he had served on. Hastily installed phones were manned by project secretaries and assistants. They were going down long lists of numbers, systematically placing calls, asking questions, giving orders. As Phillips made his way toward Darro's desk, he heard snatches of the conversations.

". . . first name Jerome, or Jerry. His photo is on the wires now. Six foot three, one eight-five pounds, dark brown hair . . ."

". . . on your international hookups, too. Include the Far East, every major travel terminal. The second man is to be considered potentially dangerous."

". . . no description other than a blue-eyed male of average appearance, six feet, about one hundred seventy-five pounds. Probably dressed in items stolen from our laboratory clothing lockers. The missing apparel . . ."

Dr. Chen bent over the desk, showing Darro the hair-implanting machine and several used cosmetic preparations. A secretary took notes in shorthand as he displayed each item.

"You see the traces of several types of medium-brown hair in the implanter."

"Be specific, Chen!" Darro snapped. "Brows, lashes, body hair . . . ?"

"Apparently following existing programming, there was normal hair distribution on the body. Scalp hair thick and curly. It also appears he—*it* used the preparations designed to simulate moles, sun wrinkles, typical epidermic imperfections. It also used a medium fair skin tone—"

Darro interrupted quickly, "Are you saying it'll look human in every way?"

"Yes, sir. As programmed."

The project chief nodded and looked questioningly at Phillips. "We have an artist's rendering being copied now for distribution," Phillips said.

"Good. We can keep to our escaped-lunatic story." Darro turned to the secretary and began to dictate further search and surveillance instructions. Phillips wondered whether it would work. The android had been programmed to look like any average American male. It was tourist season in Europe. If the android got that far, how would they find him among the millions of sightseers in vacationing crowds? Phillips doubted that even Darro was that good.

7

The jet approached Heathrow Airport in a dense fog that had Jerry's heart in his throat throughout the descent. Questor peered out the window with interest, scanning what seemed to be layer after layer of thick mist.

"Pea soup," Jerry muttered.

Questor glanced at him, head tilted questioningly to the right. "I do not analyze that substance as a comestible," he said. "It is a heavy moisture layer consisting of—"

"Questor," Jerry said patiently, "I was using a slang expression for *fog*."

"I see. My knowledge of the vernacular seems to be lacking. I trust you will help me in this area?"

"Oh sure. We'll have lots of time to review the language . . . in prison."

"I have a plan, Mr. Robinson," Questor said calmly.

Jerry nodded skeptically. "Right."

The British immigration officials were very polite, as Jerry knew they would be. They listened, without interruption, to the fabricated story about the passports in the luggage. But, of course, there was that one little hitch. There was no luggage. Questor said it was undoubtedly lost in transit. He understood that a great many suitcases were misrouted in error. The immigration officials nodded courteously and asked them to accompany the guard to the office where everything would be straightened out. Jerry began to calculate his remaining hours of freedom.

The chief immigration inspector was on the phone at his desk when the guard escorted Jerry and Questor toward his glass-walled office. "No luggage at all?" he said

into the receiver. "No baggage checked in Los Angeles
. . . no possible error? You're certain?" He listened to the
voice on the other end of the phone and nodded. "Yes.
Yes, quite interesting. Thank you." He hung up and
studied the two men being ushered in by the guard.

The taller of the two appeared to be in his late twen-
ties. He had dark hair, intelligent, lively eyes under a
high, wide forehead. At the moment, a slightly worried
frown creased the forehead, spoiling the normally cheerful, friendly face. He was a slender man, well dressed in a
black turtleneck sweater and slacks and wearing a tailored
suede jacket.

The other man was shorter but more sturdily built. He
was lighter haired and fair skinned, a man with a curiously
immobile expression. And his clothes! The inspector's
proper soul was scandalized at the sight of the open-
necked sport shirt, tweed jacket, chinos, and white socks.
He almost wished there were a dress code to enforce, but
these two were in enough trouble as it was.

He stood up, half bowing courteously. "Would you
mind terribly if there's a little delay?"

"No," Jerry said as casually as possibly. "Of course not.
Why should we mind?"

"This way, please." The immigration inspector led them
down a short corridor, the guard discreetly following in
case of trouble. They stopped at a detention-room, and
the inspector dug out a key to unlock the door. He
opened it and turned to Jerry and Questor. "Would you
mind waiting in here? You'll find it more comfortable
while we sort out some red tape."

"We will acquiesce to your request," Questor said
politely. He entered the room, and Jerry followed.

The immigration inspector closed the door behind them
and locked it. Jerry looked around the room. There wasn't
much to see. It wasn't a cell—there were comfortable
chairs and a table . . . but there were no windows. The
only other door besides the one through which they had
entered was a heavy metal fire door on the opposite wall.

Jerry turned to Questor. "You said you had a plan!"

Questor nodded and went to the fire door. It was locked

or bolted from the other side. "Since an extraterritorial investigation of this nature involves several government agencies, and thus several detention locations . . ." He systematically examined the door to determine how it was secured, then firmly grasped the top hinge ". . . we will inspect the detention potential of each until . . ." He pulled, and the top hinge twisted completely loose in his hand, accompanied by the sound of protesting metal and crumbling concrete. The door sagged. ". . . a reasonable exit is discovered." He bent and pulled free the bottom hinge, then lifted the door aside. "Logic indicates the simplest plan is usually best."

Jerry stared at the wrecked door. "It also helps if you can pull three-inch steel bolts out of reinforced concrete. Let's get out of here."

"Of course," Questor said politely. "That is my programmed imperative."

Darro was presiding over the meeting in the security conference room, and presiding with some impatience. Every new revelation caused a ripple of excitement or startled comment in the audience. They included the project scientists, intelligence personnel, and several other government representatives from the five powers. Two high-ranking generals sat in the front row, frowning as Darro spoke.

"Next, the American government has uncovered a few disturbing facts. Dr. Bradley, please?"

Phyllis Bradley rose and glanced briefly at the sheaf of reports in her hand. "Our psychologists are unanimous in the opinion that despite Robinson's intelligence, he displays a well-defined personality introversion. Dr. Chen?"

"Our doctors concur totally. It is highly unlikely that Robinson could have planned this—or even cooperated willingly."

"In short," Darro said, "it appears that the android engineered its own escape." He waited for the babble of talk to recede. "What we face, then, is an incredibly efficient machine. Its capabilities may go far beyond what we ever expected."

Gorlov hunched up to the edge of his chair suspiciously. "My government finds it hard to consider even such a clever machine to be an international crisis. You have asked to be given exceptional powers, Mr. Darro."

"I suggest to your government, Doctor, it may be crucial to find it now—while there is only *one* such machine to deal with."

The French scientist, Audret, pushed to his feet and spoke over the furor in the room. "Monsieur, it required our combined resources to build only one of them. If you are suggesting someone plans an army of such devices—"

Darro interrupted coldly. "Doctor, are you certain this machine may not be capable of reproducing itself? And there are other possibilities. We know it can change its appearance at will, perhaps to resemble any of you here, or even a national leader." He ignored the stir of voices and quieted them with the power of his own. "But the most pressing questions are *why* was it designed? *Why* was it programmed to escape? I think it's important that you now hear from someone who actually knew and worked with Dr. Vaslovik. Miss Allison Sample, his former secretary."

Allison had been seated in a corner, barely noticed by the others. At Darro's gesture, she stood and came to the podium. Darro noticed that she trembled slightly and her hands dripped with nervous perspiration. He extended himself and managed a genuinely reassuring smile for her.

"Miss Sample has been made aware of the confidential nature of this meeting. Please speak freely, Miss Sample."

She nodded, a little more sure of herself. "I'd like to make it clear I first consented to answer questions about my former employer only because of my concern for Mr. Robinson."

"Miss Sample was admirably reticent," Darro interjected. He nodded to her. "But what changed that? When Vaslovik's background records were checked—*thoroughly* checked by my people—please tell us what was discovered."

Allison bit her lip nervously. It was difficult for her to

admit the facts that Darro had shown her. How could she have worked so closely with Vaslovik and never known? She realized that the audience was waiting for her, and forced herself to speak. "Except for his scientific and academic life, almost everything else about him or his past either couldn't be verified or . . . or appeared to be totally false."

The listening group exploded in agitation again, and Darro waited for them to quiet. "Copies of that investigative report will be distributed. Miss Sample, did Professor Vaslovik seem to be concerned over the things happening in the world?"

Allison hesitated, then nodded. "Yes. Very worried."

A phone light on the table beside the podium began to flash. Phillips instantly picked it up and answered it in a low murmur.

"Could Vaslovik have dreamed of replacing the human race with something more efficient?" Darro asked.

"Mr. Darro, I . . . I can't guess at what dreams might have been in Dr. Vaslovik's mind."

Phillips urgently waved Darro to the phone. As the project chief took the receiver, Allison turned to the audience again. "The thing I thought important to tell you was that soon after the android broke out, a man came to our archives. He seemed strange at first—incredibly formal—then he became rather charming. I found later he'd broken into all our files and no one could identify him, though he *said* he was part of the project. He said *his* name was Questor."

She expected an uproar. Instead, the group fell quiet, stunned. Allison leaned forward, her voice low and earnest. "I realize now it was learning to deal with humans even while it was talking to me. I'm not saying it's dangerous. But it learns very, very fast."

Darro hung up the phone and came back to the podium. Allison stepped aside, sensing something wrong. Darro gripped the edges of the lectern so fiercely that it shook. "Ladies and gentlemen . . . I've just received word the android and Robinson were detained by British Immigration in London. No passports. They escaped from a locked room within minutes with almost ridiculous ease."

Jerry was grateful for the protection of darkness as they slipped out of the air terminal. He had managed to exchange twenty-five dollars into pounds without drawing attention to himself. Then he and Questor joined a group crowding onto the airport shuttle bus into town. Once deposited at the bus terminal, he looked around at Questor.

"All right. Now where?"

"We are not in the city center?"

"No. Wait a minute. Do you mean the *exact* center of the city, or where things are happening? Uh . . . where people congregate."

"Excellent, Mr. Robinson. You clarified your statement most precisely. I believe we should proceed toward the area where . . . things are happening."

"We'll be less noticeable in the underground then."

Questor pondered briefly. "The underground is the subway system, also called the tube."

"Now you've got it."

"I'm sure I shall find it most interesting."

They located the nearby underground entrance and descended the several flights of stairs with another group of commuters. Jerry studied the comprehensive map of the various lines and decided on the best route to Piccadilly Circus. He pointed out the stop on the map. "There ought to be plenty happening there."

Questor frowned. "Entertainment by animals and other such acts will not aid my programmed imperative."

"Questor, the word *circus* in this context doesn't mean what you think. It's difficult to explain exactly, but—" His voice was drowned out in the roar of the arriving subway train. Jerry quickly purchased tickets and guided Questor into one of the cars. Happily, the android was so fascinated by the sights, sounds, and smells of this new world that he did not pursue the matter of the word *circus*.

They exited at the Piccadilly Circus stop and emerged into a throng of evening street people. Traffic flowed endlessly around the massive fountain that was topped by the graceful statue of Eros. The traditional blaze of neon signs on every building around the great circle seared the night sky and cast strange shadows. Young people clustered at the base of the fountain, playing guitars and flutes, singing their own kind of songs. On every inch of sidewalk, people jostled one another.

Questor took it all in, fascinated. Here was a world he had not known existed—the gaps in the tapes had jumped over London's night life. Jerry guided him out of the sidewalk traffic pattern and into a quieter area beside the building.

Questor studied the street corner with great interest. "Curious. Why would that man be examining a printed facsimile of your facial components?"

Jerry jumped nervously and stared around. The uniformed man stood on the corner, holding a police sketch up to the light so that he could read it. "The bobby? You can see what he's reading from here?"

Questor looked again, his eyes automatically switching to telescopic mode, which brought in the picture and the writing as clearly as if he held the sheet himself. "Under your likeness there is printing which states you are a technician employed on a highly classified project at an American university. You are suspected of stealing a valuable computing device, and you are traveling with a highly dangerous companion. I assume this last refers to me. Several governments are offering extremely high rewards for information leading to our apprehension and arrest." He turned back to Jerry. "At the proper time, of course, I will explain that you did not steal me."

"Oh, the courts will love that! A machine testifying for the defense."

The bobby tucked away the sketch and began to study the passersby with more care. Jerry tapped Questor's arm and nudged him into a group of tourists on a sightseeing tour of the city at night. They moved past the bobby, concealed by the group. Once beyond the policeman's sight, Jerry headed down a side street which angled into Leicester Square.

"Mr. Robinson," Questor said quietly. He nodded to-

ward a corner ahead. Another bobby stood there, and he
too had a copy of the sketch. Questor and Jerry ducked
into the recessed doorway of a store.

"They want us badly."

Questor nodded and said, "I think it best, Mr. Robinson, that I proceed alone. I do not wish you harmed."

Jerry eyed him, gauging him, not understanding. "Why
not? If you can't feel, why should you care?"

Questor hesitated, considering reasons. There was only
one reasonable, ethical answer. "We had an agreement,
which you have honored. A contract is a perfectly logical
arrangement."

Jerry felt a peculiar emotion choking his throat, making
it hard for him to speak. "You know something, Questor?
I almost wish it were more."

Questor nodded. "I, too." He glanced around the corner
of the doorway and saw that the bobby had left. "Good-
bye, Mr. Robinson."

Jerry shook his head firmly. "No. I'm not going. Questor, you won't understand this because it's very, very
human . . . but this is the first time in my life I've built
something that said, 'Jerry Robinson, I need help. It's not
just enough to puzzle me out, put me together. I need
more.' Don't you see what I mean? There's more to you
than just understanding your parts. There's a whole *you*
. . . though I'm not sure what that whole you really is. I
sometimes get nervous when I try to imagine why Vaslovik designed you—" A shrill, high-pitched police whistle
interrupted him, and he looked up to see a bobby racing
diagonally across the street toward them.

"You there! Hold where you are!"

Jerry and Questor broke into a run, careening down the
street and around a corner. More whistles erupted behind
them, then were drowned out in the rising and falling wail
of a police siren. Jerry darted into a narrow cobbled alley
and led the way into a quieter side street.

He scanned left and right and saw a private casino
down the street. A uniformed doorman was busy flagging
down a cab. The man beside him swayed like a falling top,
and only the doorman's hand kept him from flopping over.

Jerry touched Questor's arm again, and the android followed him toward the casino as a taxi pulled up in answer to the doorman's signal. While the doorman was diverted putting the drunk into the cab, Jerry and Questor ducked into the club.

"I think we're safer here than on the street. But stay close to me. Be casual."

"I will follow your example," Questor said.

Jerry suddenly felt that their roles should be reversed. Questor was always calm. Jerry was dripping with sweat and slightly annoyed to notice that Questor did not even breathe hard after their crazy dash through the streets. He had to remind himself that the android was not supposed to breathe heavily after exertion—or maybe that *should* have been built into him to make him seem more human. A chilly English voice sliced into his musings.

"Sir? Do you belong to this club?"

Jerry looked around at the tuxedo-clad manager. The man was small, narrow, his triangular face only slightly balanced by a neat moustache. Discreet gold and diamond studs glimmered on his immaculate white shirt.

"Ah . . . no. You see, we're American." Jerry floundered, but then got better at fabrication as he went on. "What I mean is, we were told about the place by some friends who'd been here. Friends of *members*. And they said there was no problem about visitors . . . one time. Lend lease—something like that—you know?"

"The members' names?"

"Ah, Smith."

The manager frowned, dubious; but he finally nodded toward the main room. "Very well. One visit is permitted. Enjoy yourselves, gentlemen." He turned away and Jerry sighed in relief.

"Come on, Questor."

The casino foyer was richly decorated, but the main salon was opulent. Delicate chandeliers presided over a room whose walls were covered with flocked fabric—the windows draped in velvet. The deep carpet pile felt six inches thick. Gaming tables were heavy antique mahogany.

Even to Jerry's amateur eye, the paintings on the walls were a tasteful selection of works by master artists.

The decorations of the people in the casino were equally opulent. The women leaned toward designer gowns and a variety of gem stones in their jewelry. The men wore tuxedos and favored gold cufflinks, studs, and rings. Lovely young cocktail waitresses moved among the crowd, serving drinks. Their costumes were just barely lawful.

Questor's eyes scanned the entire room, analyzing and cataloging. People gathered around various tables playing blackjack, roulette, craps, *chemin de fer,* baccarat. The money and chips passing across the tables were high denominations. Most of it seemed to be going to the dealers.

Questor turned to Jerry with the inquisitive tilt of his head that had become a habit. "Curious. These humans proffer specie and receive nothing in return."

"They are gambling, a form of recreation." Jerry was nervous, aware of the way they stood out in the well-dressed crowd. He was not sure the casino manager believed their story, and he was afraid he would hear the shrill tweet of a police whistle at any moment.

Questor scanned around again. "Gambling . . . yes, the enjoyment of random chance." He watched a man run his fingers down the spine of his female companion, who wore a backless gown. Another man accepted a drink from the tray of a scantily clad waitress and patted her rear as she moved away. Questor frowned. "This puzzles me, too. The human males intent upon the epidermal portions of the females."

"Look, this is going to be very hard to explain to a machine. . . ."

"It is the biological continuity between male and female?"

Jerry shifted his weight uncomfortably and avoided Questor's bright, inquiring eyes. That was one way to put it, but Jerry chose to try to elucidate further. "Well . . . sort of a combination of biology and booze."

"Interesting," Questor said. "Will we observe humans mating here?"

Jerry grabbed his arm and guided him away from a couple who had heard the last question and turned to eye them curiously. "No, not here. I mean, the people here aren't involved quite that way with each other. Well, maybe they're kind of involved." He saw he had entangled himself too deeply to get out and ended lamely, "The whole thing is rather . . . involved."

Questor stared at him, and Jerry had the uneasy feeling that he was being cataloged as an idiot. But the android said nothing, instead beginning a study of the various gaming tables they passed as they toured the room. He stopped briefly at each table, following the game for a hand or a spin of the wheel, a toss of the dice.

"If there's any of this you'd like to know about . . ." Jerry began.

"I am still analyzing your last explanation, Mr. Robinson." Questor nodded toward the gaming tables. "This appears to be much simpler. Elementary mathematics." They passed a blackjack table, then Questor stopped to watch several passes at a crap table. He looked at Jerry. "As you said, we require specie—" He interrupted himself. "We need money. More colloquial?"

Jerry smiled. "Better. But I've only got twenty-six dollars left, Questor, a little over ten pounds British money. If we lose that, we're broke. I can't use my credit cards without being identified."

"If you have doubts, I have calculated the variables and will simply measure shape, weight, direction, and energy required to expose the cube faces we desire."

"Are you saying you can throw any number you want?"

"Can I expose any combination of cube faces?" He nodded and displayed his fingers. "Quite easily, by calculating the friction of the tabletop plus the angle and energy imparted to the cubes." A thought occurred to him as he studied Jerry's startled face. "Or is it immoral to use my sensory apparatus in this fashion?"

Jerry's principles shook—and succumbed. "Uh . . . no. They *do* call these 'games of skill.' " He dug out his wallet and gave Questor his money.

They angled their way into a place at the crap table.

The player rolling the dice crapped out, and the croupier collected the dice. Questor leaned in slightly. "May I participate?"

The croupier pushed the dice toward him with the stick. Questor extended the pound notes. The croupier looked at him scornfully and handed him two low-denomination chips. Questor ignored the sarcastic ripple of amusement that went around the table and put the two chips on the line. Jerry covertly nodded that this was correct.

Questor picked up the dice. His fingertip sensors transmitted the information on their weight and measurements while his eyes surveyed the table, calculating length and breadth, the friction effect of the green baize surface, the exact force of the throw required. As soon as the information computed, he positioned the dice in his right hand and tossed them out awkwardly.

The dice bounced and rolled and came up a four and a three. "Seven," said the croupier tonelessly. "Pay the line." He pushed two more chips toward Questor.

Questor examined the odds marked in the boxes on the field and nodded. "I will wager next on each cube with two dots."

"Four the hard way," the croupier said. He placed the chips on the table so the bet was correct.

Questor picked up the dice, again swiftly calculating the force, angle, and bounce needed. Then he rolled. The dice stopped with each face exposing two spots.

"Four . . . the hard way," the croupier said blandly. He had known it to happen. He began to push the chips toward Questor.

"Permit it to accumulate, please," Questor said.

"What's that?"

Jerry stepped in, smiling as appealingly as he knew how. "He means let it ride."

The croupier shrugged and began to stack the chips on the table. Questor started to position the dice in his fingers again.

Jerry nudged him discreetly and whispered, "I think you should throw something else."

Questor thought about it briefly and realized that Jerry

was correct. The mathematical odds of his rolling the same number the same way twice were quite large, therefore unbelievable to the average human. Besides, there were better odds on the table. He addressed the croupier. "May I wager it all within the rectangle labeled 'craps—eight to one'?"

The croupier stared at him, nonplussed. "Within the craps rectangle?"

Questor nodded blandly. "This is my first gambling. I find it quite interesting."

The croupier suspiciously studied Questor but finally began to put down the bet. He had decided, as had the manager, that these two were American tourists and as such were entitled to more tolerance for their madness than would normally be given.

"The gentleman says any craps."

Questor carefully positioned the dice, calculated the required measurements, and tossed the cubes. They bounced, hit the end of the table, fell back, and came up with one spot on each exposed surface.

The croupier's voice was decidedly weak. "Snake eyes."

Questor busily scanned the board. "I perceive I have made an error. I will expose the same faces for the fifteen-to-one odds."

The croupier's eyes narrowed into suspicious slits, but he moved the chips to the proper square. Jerry nervously glanced around and was horrified to see almost everyone in the casino moving toward the table to watch—including the casino manager. But before he could speak to Questor, the android had made his swift calculations and thrown the dice again.

There was a gasp from the onlookers as the dice bounced up snake eyes again. The croupier placed another large stack of chips beside the ones on the table. The denominations had grown larger.

Jerry anxiously tugged at Questor's sleeve. "That's enough. Come on."

Questor looked at him blandly. "The specie amount—" He corrected himself. "The money we have isn't enough yet." He turned back to the croupier politely. "Wager it on the . . . snake eyes again, please."

There was a mad flurry of hands reaching in to scoop their chips off the table. Luck is one thing. Tempting fate is another. Questor had the calculations down pat now and threw the dice with no hesitation. They danced across the green surface of the table and came to rest in front of the manager. Snake eyes.

The croupier and the casino manager exchanged glances in the confusion and babble of astonished chatter that went up around the table. The manager nodded almost imperceptibly.

Jerry saw it, too, and before him rose visions of muggings, of their bullet-riddled bodies found on the moors. He gripped Questor's elbow frantically. "Questor, please . . ."

"It is quite all right, Mr. Robinson. Trust me."

The croupier scooped in the dice and deftly palmed them, substituting another pair taken from a slot in the table directly in front of his belly. The move was smooth, unnoticeable unless one paid extremely close attention. He shoved the dice toward Questor with the long stick.

Questor picked them up and instantly felt the difference in them. The weight and even the shape were not quite what he had handled before. Because of the weight factor, force and angle of bounce would be negated. The only answer was to reshape them and redistribute the weight. Unobtrusively, as he scanned the table, he clenched the two cubes in his hand, exerting immense pressure on them.

"Your term for twelve?" he asked.

"Box cars," said the croupier.

"Place the entire wager on box cars, please."

The croupier did so, barely hiding a smug grin. There were no other bets on the table as Questor prepared to roll again.

He threw. The two white cubes tumbled, rolled—and settled, exposing the double sixes.

The crowd roared. The croupier and the casino manager were stunned, but there was nothing to do but pay off. The croupier began to stack large-denomination chips on the table. Jerry paled as he saw the manager nod to two large, broad men who looked very out of place in tuxedos. The gorilla cage at the zoo would have been more appropriate.

He turned to Questor in time to hear the android say, "That will be sufficient. Thank you very much."

"You're leaving?"

"I have enjoyed the experiment, but this accumulation of money is enough. Thank you."

At a signal from the manager, the croupier began to scoop the chips into a container. Two bounced off and rolled under the table. The croupier knelt and reached around under the low-slung mahogany table, but was unable to locate the chips.

"Allow me," Questor said courteously. He lifted the edge of the massive table with one hand.

The croupier dug out the dropped chips, started to climb to his feet, and stopped, staring. Questor gently lowered the table edge. Hands shaking, the croupier gathered the rest of the chips and gave them to Questor very respectfully.

"Thank you, sir."

"Thank *you* for a most informative ten minutes, seventeen seconds."

Questor and Jerry walked toward the door. The crowd had not ceased its confused and amazed chatter. Jerry wondered how they would break the news of his death to his mother. Then he saw the two gorillas respectfully move to one side and let them go to the cashier's window. The chips were exchanged quickly for pound notes, and no one bothered them as they left.

Jerry stopped five blocks away from the casino, looked back to see if they had been followed, and relaxed, relieved to see no one behind them. He leaned against a lamp post to gulp in refreshing breaths of crisp night air as if he had been holding his breath too long. He had.

Questor watched him, puzzled. "You appear to be suffering some strain, Mr. Robinson."

"Questor . . . do you realize that run of 'luck' you had in there could have gotten us killed? I told you to stop."

"I would have endangered your life because I changed the structure of the strange pair of dice they gave me on the last wager?"

"Strange pair of—? Questor, they gave you a *different* pair of dice? Heavier than the others?"

"Yes. But I corrected the obvious imbalance."

Jerry leaned his head back against the lamp post and began to laugh softly. Questor tilted his head slightly to the right, frowning. "This is humorous?"

"Well, yes. You see, those dice were supposed to make you lose. I'll bet they're going crazy trying to figure out how you did it."

"Was it immoral for me to do so?"

Jerry paused, thinking it over. Then he looked at Questor seriously. "No, Questor. Giving you the loaded dice was immoral. And the price they paid was heavy enough." He straightened up, much more cheerful. "But if we ever get to Vegas, there are some slot machines I want you to meet."

8

They walked a great deal that night. Jerry had begun to feel the lack of sleep and the effects of tension. Questor, who was tireless, obligingly stopped whenever Jerry's energy flagged too much, and they sat for a while. They had been too late to even try to book a room in a hotel, so they simply kept moving through London's dimly lighted streets. No one bothered them, not even the occasional bobby walking his beat. Apparently, not all the Metropolitan Police had gotten the "wanted" sheet on them.

It was almost dawn when they reached the embankment along the Thames. Jerry slumped down on a low cement wall and Questor quietly sat beside him. The slowly brightening sky had become silver gray, casting gleaming sparks of light on the broad river. Questor looked around, interested, unquenchably curious.

"Do you know where we are, Mr. Robinson?"

Jerry roused himself to study the surroundings and nodded. "This is the Thames River, London's principal waterway. The area behind us is called the embankment. It runs all the way up into Chelsea, that way." He pointed upriver. "Down there . . . those buildings are the houses of Parliament. The prominent tower with the clock is Big Ben."

"Thank you, Mr. Robinson. However, am I not correct in saying it is the large bell in the clock tower that is named Big Ben?"

Jerry sighed wearily. "Yes."

"There are other bells in the city with names equally famous, I believe. I have references to Great Peter and—"

"Yes, Questor. That's right. If you don't mind, I'm just

not up to a lecture on famous bells of the city of London right now."

"I apologize, Mr. Robinson. I did not take into account your fatigue, which would naturally blunt intellectual curiosity. Would you care to lie down on the grass to rest?"

Jerry wished he could, but practical considerations kept intruding. "We'd probably be arrested as vagrants. We can't risk that." He started to get up. "We'd better move on." He shivered in the damp morning air, suddenly aware of the vast climate difference between southern California and London.

Questor noticed the chattering of Jerry's teeth. "You are cold. I have no need of this jacket if you would care to use it."

"No, no. I'm fine."

Questor put a hand under his elbow, and Jerry sleepily allowed that firm support to propel him along. They walked up toward Chelsea, covering the distance slowly. It was just past seven when Questor turned into a narrow side street lined with Georgian-style buildings. Once they had been private residences. Now they were bed-and-breakfast hotels. Questor guided Jerry toward a woman who was briskly sweeping the steps and sidewalk in front of one of the hotels.

"Pardon me," Questor said.

The woman turned and eyed the two men. The one who had spoken was dressed in an odd assortment of clothing, but he appeared to be bright eyed, fresh, and alert. The taller man was considerably rumpled, puffy eyed, and he had a tendency to sway to the right if his companion did not hold him up.

"Can I help you?"

"I believe you can," Questor said. He pointed to a sign in the front window. "Do you have a room we could rent?"

"How long would you be staying?"

"I believe one day should be long enough. You see," Questor went on, "we arrived from the United States late last night, and our luggage was lost. We require a place

to stay until the airline can return it to us. They've promised it will not be more than a day."

"Well, I suppose that would be all right. Come along,
I'll show you the room. It's two pounds the night."

"Am I correct in assuming that includes breakfast?"

"Yes. Did you want something now?"

"I believe Mr. Robinson will appreciate some food.
Scrambled eggs, toast, butter and jam, bacon, and coffee
if you have it."

"Yes, sir." The woman led them into the house and
directed them to a sunny dining room where tables were
set and waiting. Two early risers had taken seats, and
Questor chose a table near the window and away from the
others.

Jerry slumped into a chair and stretched his long legs.
"Questor, you're getting too good at lying."

"The fabrication of a harmless story is not immoral.
You have done it, so it cannot be."

Jerry thought about it and bobbed his head. "All right,
I'll concede the point. But it has to be a *harmless* story."

"Agreed."

The woman brought in a tray and set down two plates
of eggs and bacon. Questor looked at the food, then at
Jerry, who had begun to eat immediately. He copied the
way Jerry used fork and knife, putting the food in his
mouth, chewing, swallowing. His system did not require it
for fuel, of course, but it was absorbed and utilized without waste.

Someone had left the *London Times* on a nearby table,
and Questor picked it up and began to scan it. Jerry continued to attack the food on his plate. Questor turned to
the financial section and studied the columns. Jerry paused
in the middle of the eggs and toast and stared at the
android.

"How did you know what to order?"

"I do not understand."

"Scrambled eggs, bacon, all this. How did you know
it's my favorite breakfast?"

Questor frowned, running back over data to locate the
information. "This was in my creator's programming. It is

not directly linked to you, but rather is indicated as a completely acceptable standard meal to order."

Jerry pushed aside his cleaned plate and leaned back tiredly. "Questor, I've got to get some sleep."

"We have a room here. I'm sure it will be sufficient."

The room at the top of a narrow, steep stairway was plain, but clean and comfortable. A draped window looked out over a row of other high roofs. One wall was dominated by a large fireplace that housed a gas heater controlled by a coin meter. The double bed had an ornate brass headboard, plump pillows, and a bright yellow coverlet. Jerry paid no attention to the old-fashioned wallpaper, the big mahogany wardrobe, and the fluted glass shades on the two small bedside lamps. He flopped down on the bed and heaved a sigh of relief and pleasure.

"Heaven," he said.

"I trust two hours will be sufficient?"

Jerry peered at him through red-veined eyes. "Surely you jest." He paused and shook his head. "No, I suppose you don't. Questor, human beings need more rest than that."

"I understand, but this creates a difficulty."

"If I don't get some sleep, it's going to create death."

"I have certain tasks to perform." Questor paced away and stood staring out the window, his back to Jerry.

"Questor?" Jerry said drowsily, "Something I've been wondering about . . ."

"Yes?"

"How'd you get past the airport metal detectors? Your whole skeleton . . ."

Questor did not look around. "There is a shield built into the subcutaneous skin layer. My creator anticipated the problem of such modern devices. I find Vaslovik anticipated many things. These tasks I must perform are somehow related to my locating him. One seems to lead inexorably to the next. It is almost as if he left a map for me in the programming. But, of course, certain portions of it have been obliterated." He turned to find Jerry sound asleep. "Mr. Robinson?"

Jerry did not move. His breathing was steady and quite

natural for a man deep in sleep. Questor considered the situation for a moment, then moved to the bed. He bent one of the thin decorative strips from the headboard down and around Jerry's left wrist. It formed an effective manacle, not uncomfortable, but unbreakable. Jerry would not be able to go far, even if he woke from his exhausted sleep. Questor took the afghan throw folded at the foot of the bed and placed it over Jerry. The young engineer did not stir. Questor left quietly, locking the door behind him.

The London Stock Exchange had all the turmoil and din of any place dealing in the turnover of enormous amounts of money, paper, and other negotiables. The fact that the figures were called out in well-modulated British accents made no difference in the frantic pace. Questor watched the activity on the board from the gallery, and his hypersensitive ears picked up the bids, isolating them and the effect they had on the listed stocks. He made brief notes, jotting figures on a pad. He did not need the references himself, but they would be necessary to the broker he had chosen to handle the transactions he had in mind.

Francis Scott Campbell had a reputation in brokerage for scrupulous honesty and the ability to handle complex transactions efficiently. He was the epitome of conservative dress and demeanor as he sat behind a desk that held an orderly clutter of papers and files. He waited for the strangely attired young man opposite him to state his business. Campbell fully expected it would take less than five minutes to hear him out and then tell him it was impossible for him to handle small, odd-lot transactions.

Questor leaned across the desk to hand Campbell the detailed list he had written out. "You will, if you please, follow the directions outlined there—buying and selling at the exact moments indicated." He reached into an accord'on folder he had purchased and drew out several flat sheaves of large-denomination bills. "Eighteen hundred fifty British pounds. That should be sufficient for the initial investment."

Campbell studied the list, and his eyebrows arched up

in surprise. He struggled to recover his composure, but
failed completely. "Sir, if you insist on throwing away
your money, why not just hand it out to the deserving
poor? This list is . . . well, sir, I know our markets, and I
am afraid—"

Questor interrupted quietly. "If you will follow those
directions to the letter, please? I will return this afternoon."

Campbell sighed and lifted his hand in a gesture of sur-
render. "Very well, sir. It *is* your money . . . for the next
few minutes."

Questor calculated the time required to complete the
transactions he had laid out and decided he could allow
himself the luxury of an exploratory walk alone. He did
not consider the possibility of police discovery imminent,
especially if he were not accompanied by Robinson.

He walked at a steady pace that allowed him to blend
with the passersby and yet take in everything around him.
He cataloged them all—the traffic, the merchants, the
pretty women, the predatory men, the masses of humanity
—rude, jostling, bound up in their own lives and problems,
all fascinating. Tiring of crowds, he turned off the main
thoroughfare into the quieter side streets. He noticed a
sign that read Soho, but it meant nothing in particular to
him.

Several young women lounged along the street, apparently with no destination, for he noticed they wandered
only a block or two and then turned back again. One of
them looked him over as he approached and stepped
out into his path.

"Pardon me," he said and started to go around her.

"Hello there, handsome," she said.

He stopped and studied her quizzically. No one had yet
addressed him as handsome. In fact, he did not consider
himself in those terms. The woman was dressed in a style
that was youthful, if one believed the fashion ads. Questor
noted that she was no longer truly youthful, but she did
have a supremely well-endowed figure. Questor also noticed that her face makeup was a bit too heavy, a touch

too gaudy, and decided her cosmetologist had not advised her well. Still, that was no reason to be impolite.

He nodded courteously. "Good afternoon, madam."

"Is that some kind of a joke?"

"I beg your pardon?"

She laughed brightly, with only a touch of a false note, and touched his arm playfully. "Oh, you Americans! Always the ones with the little jokes. Say, you want to have a good time?"

Questor considered the time element and realized he had an hour and forty minutes before he was due back at Campbell's office. "I see no objection to a pleasant interlude. When shall we begin?"

The woman stared at him, her dark eyebrows arching up toward her dyed black hairline. He couldn't be that dumb—could he? Even if he were, something was intensely intriguing in the steady blue eyes leveled on her, something fascinating in the impression of quiet power within him.

"I don't think you get it. You give me fifteen pounds . . . and I'll make you happy."

Questor tilted his head to the right, puzzled. "Please explain why I should become happy if I give you fifteen pounds."

"Hey, are you kidding?"

"It would, perhaps, gratify my charitable impulses—but at the moment, I am aware of none."

"Ten pounds."

"Madam, I have no wish to disappoint you, and I appreciate your desire to make me happy, but I do not understand the price scale."

She sighed. "All right. Seven pounds. But only because it's a slow day."

"But surely seven pounds would not cause the day to pass any faster."

She rolled her eyes up to heaven. Why? Why did this kind have to wander down her side of the street? Maybe if she explained. She beckoned him closer and reached up on tiptoes to whisper in his ear. Then she stepped back and smiled winningly. "You have to admit I'm pretty good-looking."

"My standards of comparison are limited, madam, but you seem quite handsome. However—"

She interrupted flatly. "Five pounds. That's as far as I can go."

"I am sure you must be correct, but as for your suggestion, I suspect there might be some technical difficulties. Still, our conversation has been most illuminating. Good day." He politely inclined his head and walked on.

The woman stared at him, her mouth starting to sag open. Then she cast a quick scan over herself in a storefront mirror. Her makeup was perfect, her hair was combed, the clothes did all the right things for her figure— or vice versa. What was *wrong* with him? "Americans," she sniffed, but she looked after his retreating back wistfully and wondered what would have happened if she'd had no price on her.

Francis Scott Campbell had seldom been surprised in his career. Events followed perfectly predictable and totally reasonable patterns, and he preferred it that way. His absolute calm had not been shaken even by the retreat from Dunkirk or the collapse of a house around him in the blitz. But the strangely dressed American he saw approaching his office for the second time that day had rattled him to his core. He struggled to his feet as Questor entered. "Mr. Questor ... I ..."

"Do you have it?"

Campbell turned to a wall safe behind his desk and worked the combination with trembling fingers. "You understand this is quite unprecedented in the annals of our stock exchange."

"Precedents are interesting, but not of immediate importance, Mr. Campbell," Questor said. "You have the entire amount in cash?"

"As requested." Campbell opened the safe and drew out a long, slim metal box. He set it on his desk and opened it to reveal neat packets of pound notes. "Three hundred thousand pounds."

"Plus seven hundred fifty-two, I believe," Questor said.

Campbell paused in taking the sheaves of notes from the box and stared at him. "Yes, precisely. Would you mind telling me—?"

"Fascinating hobby, mathematics," Questor said quickly. "I will take fifty thousand with me. It will be necessary for other business I must transact." He reached into his breast pocket and drew out another carefully printed list. "You will retain the balance and reinvest it according to these instructions. You will conduct each transaction at the exact hour and day prescribed."

Campbell took the proffered list and glanced over it. He had never seen such an assortment of proposed transactions, obscure stocks and well-known ones. There did not seem to be a system. "Mr. Questor, would you mind telling me how you . . . how you . . ."

"I thought about it," Questor answered vaguely.

Campbell sat down heavily behind his desk. Forty years in this business had not given him the incredible insight this strange American had. It was uncanny—and illogical —but it worked.

Questor gathered up his fifty thousand pounds and placed the rest of the money in Campbell's box. "I trust your fee in these transactions is recompense enough for the trouble of being so extremely correct and careful?"

"Oh, the commission is most equitable, sir."

"Good." Questor nodded. "You will continue as instructed until you hear from me." He tucked the money in his pocket, shook hands with Campbell, and left. Francis Scott Campbell was sure he would never have a more naive client—nor a more successful one.

Jerry Robinson woke from his deep sleep and tried to roll over. It was impossible; something held his left arm securely. He peered at his wrist and made out the handcuff Questor had devised. "Questor!" he shouted. He tried to wriggle around on the bed to get into a position to free himself, but this, too, was impossible. *"Questor!"*

The door opened with a rattle of the key, and the android stepped inside. "A little less noise, please, Mr.

Robinson. We do not wish to draw attention to ourselves."

"Let me out of this . . . thing."

"Of course." Questor moved to the side of the bed and
effortlessly bent back the piece of metal, freeing Jerry's
wrist. Jerry rubbed his arm briskly, trying to restore circulation, as Questor straightened the metal and pushed
it into its former position. "I am truly sorry if I caused you
any discomfort. I trust you understand my position."

"Your position! What about the one you left me in? I
may never use my arm again." He stood up, angry and
annoyed, moving his arm around to work out the stiff-
ness. "Where have you been?"

"I had a commercial transaction to complete—and I
took several hours to study the rather peculiar ways of
the human species."

"Did it ever occur to you that you might be considered
pretty peculiar yourself?"

"That would depend upon the standard of comparison,
Mr. Robinson."

Jerry stopped rubbing his arm and stared at Questor.
Why did the android have to be so damn logical all the
time? But, of course, he was programmed to be just that.
More and more often, Jerry was overlooking the fact that
Questor was a machine. Still, he said things Jerry could
not afford to overlook. "Questor, you said something
about commercial transactions?"

"Yes. I invested some of our casino winnings in the
stock market."

Jerry sat down abruptly, his knees weak. "The stock
market?"

"Yes. A rather fascinating enterprise I would like to
study further. However, for our purposes, only a brief review of its general principles was necessary."

"I see. How much . . ." Jerry paused, afraid to go
further, but he had to. "How much did you invest?"

"All of it, except for the taxi fare I paid to get to the
stock exchange."

"How much did you lose?"

"Ah, Mr. Robinson, you have so little faith in your

creation. The profit came to over three hundred thousand pounds, most of which I have reinvested for our future use." He brought out the two packets of pound notes and held them out to Jerry. "We will have need of this fifty thousand pounds for expenses. I believe you should handle it."

Jerry took the money cautiously, as if afraid it would dissolve in his hands. When it did not, he tucked it away in his breast pocket. "You know something, Questor . . . I wish I had created you instead of merely following the blueprints."

"Why do you say that?"

"You're, well, you're a fine piece of work."

Questor nodded. "I am gratified you agree I am functioning well. It is difficult for me to know at times."

"Me, too, Questor." He sighed a little and stretched. "What's next?"

"I believe a trip to the country is in order."

The home office undersecretary was waiting in a chauffeured limousine when the sleek private jet landed at Heathrow. As soon as the plane rolled to a halt, the chauffeur guided the limousine up to the set of stairs being wheeled into place by airport technicians. A pair of London police vehicles followed the official car.

Darro stepped out of the plane, followed by members of his staff. He paused at the top of the stairs and looked down, frowning deeply at the undersecretary and his assistant, two police supervisors, and several uniformed policemen who were converging on the plane. He didn't like the idea of the government *and* the police getting into this. The more people who knew the real facts, the greater chance of the truth getting out and causing a panic. He braced himself and moved down the steps.

"Mr. Darro?" said the undersecretary. When Darro nodded, the official held out his hand. "Culwait, home office undersecretary. May we talk privately a moment?"

Darro bobbed his head in the briefest of nods. Culwait led him several yards away from the others and lowered his voice as he spoke. "I'm instructed to inform you the government will cooperate fully on one condition—that there must, under no circumstances, ever be a mention of the word 'robot.' "

Darro smiled coldly. Remarkable how certain minds seem to run in the same patterns. "I understand. The risk of what it might do is far less important than the risk of bringing down the party in power."

Culwait drew himself up in annoyance, and his voice grew ponderous with dignity. "Our concern happens to be for public safety, Darro. We are simply nervous over the possible panic—"

"—which the word 'robot' would create among the labor bloc," Darro interrupted. "I've gotten the same message from the other governments." He permitted himself the slight bend of his mouth that served as a smile. "Which makes me certain you'll cooperate in every way, no matter what I ask. You have no choice."

He turned and walked away, back to his staff. Culwait glared after him angrily. No wonder Darro had been chosen to head up so many national and international projects. He had a personality like a sledgehammer—and about as much in the way of diplomacy. A man like that had to be honest to stay alive.

9

The London cab cruised along the country road at a modest speed, and Questor's head never seemed to stop moving as he took in the scenery. Jerry sat in a corner of the wide back seat, glumly staring out at the green hedges and meadows at the roadside. The cabbie had more important things to watch . . . oncoming drivers and a meter that read over thirty-two pounds and was still climbing. He glanced back at the two men and cleared his throat nervously.

"It's a bit of a bill you're runnin' up, gentlemen."

"Our journey will terminate in precisely three-tenths of a mile."

The cab driver nodded dubiously. That did not answer the question of whether or not they could pay the tab, but they seemed to know where they were going. Presumably, they also anticipated the size of the bill.

Jerry leaned over to Questor confidentially. "What do we ask for when we get where we're going?"

"C."

Jerry blinked. " 'C'?"

"This entire portion of my creator's records was cryptographically encoded to resemble casual social notes."

"Code?" Jerry hissed. "What kind of business did he do with this C?"

"Principally information exchange on international matters."

"Questor, we can't just knock at a door and ask for a code name which . . ." He trailed off as he noticed the private drive the cab was traversing.

A long, tree-lined drive threaded its way through a cleft

in natural rock and then burst out into an open expanse of lawn that was dotted with carefully planned flower beds. The house that rose at the end of the drive was vast, classic in style, ancient stone only lightly touched by modern architects on the outside. This was the first genuine stately mansion Jerry had ever seen.

"Questor," he said weakly, "especially not on the door of *that* house."

The cabbie pulled up before the massive main door and stopped. Jerry stepped out, still taking in the immensity of the house, the obviously expensive setting. He turned back to find Questor handing a thick wad of pound notes to the driver. "Wait, Questor. We may need him."

Questor ignored him and nodded to the cabbie. "You may go now."

The driver ran a finger through the stack of bills and figured out the large tip. "That's very generous, gov'nor. Thank ya kindly." He drove away, and Questor turned to Jerry.

"I am convinced you will not fail me, Mr. Robinson."

Jerry had no answer for that kind of remark. He and Questor approached the heavy door, and Jerry lifted and dropped the ornate knocker almost timidly. Questor's eyes flicked around the entrance area and stopped on what appeared to be an ornamentally carved projection in the architecture.

"Curious. It appears we are being scanned by an electronic camera device."

Jerry frowned doubtfully. "I don't see anything. How can you tell?"

Questor promptly reached up to the projection, twisted, and revealed the end of a closed-circuit television camera aimed at where they were standing. Jerry waggled a hand anxiously.

"Put it back . . . quick!"

Questor complied, just getting the decorative cover back on the lens as the door opened. A formally attired butler stared out at them inquiringly.

Jerry looked at Questor, but Questor waited for him. "Ah . . . tell your . . . uh, master, that . . ."

The butler started to close the door. Questor still made no move, and Jerry jumped forward in time to get his foot in the door and push it open again. The cold disdain of the butler had started to annoy him. "Listen, I clearly said 'tell your master . . .' "

The butler interrupted contemptuously. "There *is* no master, sir." He tried to close the door again, but Jerry held it open.

"Then tell whoever that we're here to talk to C about Vaslovik."

Unblinkingly, the butler scanned them, but a slight frown indicated that he was undecided. Finally he opened the door all the way and gestured them in with a tiny wave. "I shall inquire of Lady Helena if that message is of any interest."

"Lady Helena?" Robinson said.

"Lady Helena Alexandre Trimble, sir." The butler turned and moved up a marble staircase that circled up to the second floor. Jerry stared after him, alarmed.

"Questor, Helena Trimble is world . . . world infamous. Vaslovik couldn't possibly have had anything to do with—"

Jerry bit off his words when a capable-looking, cold-eyed man appeared at the bottom of the short flight of stairs leading to the main room. To Jerry, he looked broad as a door and quite out of place in a conservatively cut business suit. The man ignored Jerry and Questor, but took a chair positioned exactly where he could keep an eye on them and be ready for anything they might attempt. Jerry did not like the way the man's jacket bulged out slightly precisely where a shoulder holster would be. Then he noticed Questor's head swivel toward the head of the stairs, and he followed the android's look.

Lady Helena Alexandre Trimble was as beautiful and as expensive as the surroundings. The pale blue culottes, topped by a matching bolero sweater trimmed with pearls, served to emphasize her height, her perfect figure, her dark hair and exquisite beauty. She had been about to make an entrance, an aloof smile on her lovely lips. But the smile froze as she stared down at the two men at the foot of the stairs. A slight, puzzled frown flickered across her face as she held Questor's look for a long moment. There was something about him . . . something both strange and familiar . . . she could not define it, but it was troubling. She gathered her composure and moved down the stairs in a flowing, floating motion, trailing one hand on the marble banister.

Jerry watched her, stunned into silence by her poise, her sensual beauty, and the fact that she could not seem to remove her eyes from Questor. Questor, on the other hand, merely waited. It was up to Jerry to make the explanations, and he was not sure he had the savoir faire to carry off conversational gambits with this woman.

"Ah . . . madam . . . I mean, Lady Helena . . ." She looked at him, waiting, dark eyes inquisitive. He pulled himself together and began again. "I'm Jerry Robinson. This is my . . . friend, Mr. Questor."

Questor snapped a look at him, his head tilted to the right in the questioning attitude he affected. Jerry Robinson had just said something Questor had never heard before.

"Randolph said you wished to discuss a matter of some importance," Lady Helena said.

"Yes. Uh . . . we're looking for an Emil Vaslovik. Can you help us?"

Lady Helena's face remained completely beautiful and completely devoid of expression. "Vaslovik? I do not know such a name." She started to turn away, down the stairs.

"Are you certain, madam? It's very important to my friend that—"

Lady Helena looked back, her voice an icy dagger. "I am not accustomed to having my word questioned, sir."

Her tone nearly riveted Jerry to the floor, but he glanced at Questor and saw a look of disappointment on his usually expressionless face, which gave him the nerve to go on. "My friend isn't often that wrong, madam. I think you do know Vaslovik."

"Mueller."

Lady Helena's voice instantly galvanized the man at the

foot of the stairs. He got to his feet and moved toward them, his hand automatically going into his jacket toward the shoulder holster.

Jerry nervously turned to Questor. "Maybe if you tell her what you saw in Vaslovik's files . . ."

Questor nodded and began his recital. "There were many coded references to a person known as C who lives in this domicile, madam. Information exchanges regarding the affairs of various nations, secret treaties, diplomatic agreements, weapons systems, specifics on certain personal idiosyncrasies of political leaders."

Lady Helena's expression did not change, but she turned abruptly to Mueller and waved him away. "That will be all, Mueller."

The strong-arm man nodded mutely and left. Robinson stared at Questor, startled by the last revelation. He edged over to the android and whispered urgently, "Secret agreements, weapons systems—you never mentioned that."

Questor's voice boomed out normally. "You never requested specifics, Mr. Robinson." He ignored Jerry's frantic gestures to keep his voice down and continued in the same tone to Lady Helena. "For example, in the area of political-leader idiosyncrasy—item: Monsieur Vardon of the Foreign Ministry of France, as regards the wife of his young second assistant, Monsieur—"

Lady Helena interrupted coolly. "I know nothing about any such 'coded' information, gentlemen."

Questor reached into his pocket and held out a small slip of paper. "You will recognize the name of the brokerage firm. Several hours ago, a small block of stock was purchased in your name. You have in your hand the identifying code number. If you will speak to a certain Francis Scott Campbell, he will verify the account."

She took the slip and stared at the number written on it. "The office will be closed at this hour."

"Mr. Campbell is waiting for your call."

Her hand trembled slightly, and she folded the paper to hide it. "I realize I've been inexcusably rude. May I ask you to wait just a moment or two, and I'll have Randolph escort you to the terrace. You will stay for a drink?"

"Yes . . . yes, thank you," Jerry said hastily. He added a smile as an afterthought.

She nodded briefly and turned away, almost gliding down the steps to the main floor, and went into a secluded room. She leaned against the door as it shut behind her, glanced at the paper in her hand, and saw her hand begin to shake again. This had happened once before—she remembered it all—but there was a part to be played, in case this man who called himself Questor was not who she thought he was. A delicate white French-style phone stood on the table beside her. She picked up the receiver and dialed the number on the paper. It was answered almost immediately.

"Mr. Campbell . . . this is account number 9077694. I believe a purchase was made for me a few hours ago in the amount of one thousand pounds. Would you mind—" She stopped, listening, not surprised at what Francis Scott Campbell was saying. "Fifty thousand pounds," she repeated. "Yes, please continue to follow the instructions left you. Thank you." She hung up and stood for a moment, staring at the phone. Then she lifted it and began to dial again.

Jerry was restless and nervous and more than a little troubled. As soon as Lady Trimble was out of sight, he turned to the android. "Questor, that information adds up to espionage, blackmail, maybe worse. Are you absolutely certain you don't know what you were designed for?"

"That was obviously among the erased information, Mr. Robinson."

"But it could mean you were designed for immoral purposes. Remember, you promised you would let me guide you in that area."

Questor turned his solemn blue eyes on Jerry and bobbed his head in a short nod. "As long as your advice does not conflict with the imperatives from my creator, Mr. Robinson."

Jerry stared at him, still troubled. Questor was picking

up more and more human habits and mannerisms. He
certainly knew how to lie, and Jerry was not sure that the
android knew the distinction between a little white lie and
one that concealed facts which Jerry had to know.

Lady Helena came to the foot of the stairs, the butler
trailing after her. A frown creased her lovely forehead,
and she studied the two men carefully before she spoke.
"Are you aware you're being sought by the police?"

"Perfectly," said Questor.

"Would you mind explaining how you just learned
that?" Jerry asked.

Lady Helena smiled for the first time, a reassuring
smile. "You needn't worry—you're quite safe here." She
turned to Questor, apparently fascinated by him in some
strange way. "Tell me, why is locating this . . . Vaslovik
so important to you, Mr. Questor?"

"It is vital I find him, madam, since—"

Jerry stepped in, interrupting Questor's attempt to tell
the truth. "Since Dr. Vaslovik is as near to a father as
Mr. Questor ever had, Lady Helena."

Her eyes searched Questor's face for any glimmer of
expression that would suggest that that was a lie. Questor
stared back levelly, openly. In fact, she had begun to see
more and more in him that was appealing. "Well," she
said, and found a warm smile for them, "it's late in the
day for such a long journey back to London." She turned
to the butler. "Randolph, our guests will stay overnight.
See if you can provide them with some fresh clothing."

Randolph bowed his way past her. "Yes, madam. This
way, gentlemen." He led them up the wide curving stairway to the second floor.

The guest room was actually two bedrooms with a sitting room between them. The decor was rich, not ostenta-
tious. Most of the furniture was antique; the colors of the
carpets, drapes, and wallpaper were soft and complemen
tary. Jerry peered into a wall mirror and carefully knotted
his tie. He had been given a handsome gray pinstripe
suit, a white shirt, and a maroon tie. He had briefly wondered how Lady Trimble happened to have a tailored suit

on hand that exactly fit a six-foot-three-inch, one-hundred-eighty-five-pound man—and then decided he did not want to speculate. Questor, too, had been given clothing precisely cut to fit him. At the moment, he was struggling to get the black and gold "school tie" into place, and not making any progress. He also had a lot of questions to ask.

"Then Lady Helena is reputed to be a courtesan? As described in some works of de Maupassant?"

"At a much higher level than that. And it's pretty clear now why she moves in those circles." He finished with his tie and turned toward Questor, folding his collar down into place and reaching for the suit coat. "Questor, even if she would help us, we couldn't afford her!"

"That statement is currently inaccurate, Mr. Robinson. But according to de Maupassant, the human female can be persuaded in ways far more powerful than the simple exchange of money."

"Well, yes, I suppose, given the right relationship, any woman could be convinced there's more to life than money, but . . ."

Questor continued to fuss and work the tie around, peering past Jerry into the wall mirror as he spoke. "Then a most logical course now would be for you to establish such a relationship with Lady Helena."

"What?"

"I have no other source of information but her. Please help me." He turned to Jerry, pleading.

Jerry automatically reached out and began to tie the intractable school tie for him. "I'd like to, but this particular human female isn't the average human female."

"Since we first met," Questor said, "I have observed expertise in many areas where you doubted yourself. And all my data tapes indicate that this should be a most pleasant experience for you. Please help me, my . . ." He paused and looked at Jerry, who had neatly finished knotting the tie in place and had stepped back. "Is it permissible to call you my friend? Earlier you called me the same."

Jerry looked at him for a long moment, then he sighed

and nodded. "I did call you that, didn't I? That's how I'm beginning to think of you. Funny."

"It is amusing to be friends with a machine, Mr. Robinson?"

"No . . . it's not amusing at all." Jerry smiled warmly, genuinely. "And, as friends, you should call me Jerry."

"My friend . . . Jerry," Questor said slowly. He thought it over, liking the sound of it—and liking Jerry's friendly grin. Then he briskly turned back to business. "Will you establish the necessary relationship with Lady Helena, my friend Jerry?"

Jerry snapped a sharp look at him, then muttered, "Checkmate."

Questor tilted his head to the right, puzzled. "Checkmate . . . a reference to the game named chess?"

"Also a reference to being had," Jerry said ruefully. "You're getting good, Questor."

"Good at what?"

"Conning people."

"I do not understand that reference."

Jerry shrugged into his jacket. "Maybe I'll explain it to you someday—but by then you'll probably have figured it out."

10

The dining room was equipped with a table that would comfortably seat twenty. Jerry felt rather lonely seated at one end of the long table with Lady Helena and Questor. The dining room itself was pure elegance in muted tones of gold and white. An overhead chandelier shed soft light down on the Limoges china, the delicate crystal, the heavy silver flatware. Fresh flowers sent forth a gentle, sweet scent from their position as centerpiece. The food had been excellent, served silently and efficiently by two maids and a waiter under Randolph's direction.

Conversation had been general, with Jerry and Lady Helena doing most of the talking. Questor had remained silent, concentrating on the food, interjecting only an occasional remark as Jerry answered Lady Helena's questions about his background and career. She revealed little of herself but spoke knowledgeably about music, literature, history, and the world in general. Jerry had even begun to relax by the time the main course was ready to be cleared away.

"The chicken cacciatore was delicious, Lady Helena," he said as he laid his napkin beside his plate.

She smiled graciously. "I'm glad you enjoyed it, Mr. Robinson." She looked over at Questor. "And you, Mr. Ques . . ." Her voice faded, followed by her smile as she stared at Questor's completely cleaned plate.

Questor followed Jerry's action and set his linen napkin beside his plate as he said, "Savory, madam."

The waiter stepped up beside Questor to clear away the plates. The man stopped, puzzled, starting at Questor's dish. It was clean. Where were the bones? Chicken cacciatore had bones in it. The waiter looked around the spot-less table, then under the table. Questor watched him quizzically, not understanding the man's distress. To him, and his stomach furnace, matter was matter. He had simply eaten the bones, not noticing that Jerry and Lady Helena had not. The waiter was now crawling around on the floor. Where the hell were the *bones?*

Lady Helena stood abruptly, covering the moment, even though she, too, wondered about the disappearing chicken bones. "Shall we have dessert and coffee on the terrace?"

Questor and Jerry came to their feet as she rose, but Jerry almost sat down again when Questor spoke. "If you will excuse me, I have matters which require attention. And I am sure you will enjoy the company of Mr. Robinson, who is an exceptional human male." He nodded politely to her and left.

Jerry smiled weakly at Lady Helena. She merely held out a hand toward the doors leading out to the terrace. "This way, Mr. Robinson."

Randolph had set up a serving cart with a silver coffee service, cups and saucers, and a freshly baked cake ready to be cut. Lady Helena accepted a cup of coffee from him, but waved away the cake for the moment. She waited as Jerry received his cup of coffee and dumped both cream and sugar into it. Perhaps he *was* as interesting as Questor had said. The memory of Questor's statement and Jerry's startled reaction to it brought a gentle smile to her lips. " 'An exceptional human male.' It must be gratifying to be called that, Mr. Robinson." She led the way toward the wall at the end of the terrace, which overlooked another, lower garden. Jerry followed her, uncertainly.

"I . . . would be more gratified if you'd call me Jerry, Lady Helena."

She smiled over her shoulder at him. "If I can be Helena to you, Jerry."

They reached the waist-high quarrystone wall overlook-ing the abundantly flowering garden below. The night was clear, the sky glittering with stars, no moon. It was still comfortably warm on the terrace, sheltered as it was by the great house. In the far distance, the lights of London cast a pale glow toward the sky. Helena looked even more exquisite than she had this afternoon. Her hair had been pulled back trimly into a French twist, held in place by a diamond hair clip. A white knit gown, simply cut and beautiful on her slim figure, needed no jewelry to enhance it. She wore an emerald ring on her right hand and a plain gold band on the ring finger of her left hand. Jerry wondered about that; but as far as he had ever heard, Lady Trimble was not married.

Jerry took a deep breath, put his cup and saucer down on the stone balustrade, and turned to her. "Helena . . . to be here with a superbly beautiful woman like you, tonight . . . the fragrance of flowers . . . this incredible view . . ." He swept his hand around and knocked the cup and saucer flying. It shattered on the stones below, and Jerry cringed.

Helena felt Jerry's embarrassment and mortification instantly and turned to him. "I'm delighted you did that," she said cheerfully. "I detest this china pattern." She tossed her own cup and saucer over the wall and listened to it smash below.

Jerry hesitated, studying her. She was so unlike what he had thought she would be. He decided to try again. "Helena, it's not often in a man's lifetime that he meets a woman who . . . who . . ." He stopped and started over. "I mean, like you and I here . . ."

Helena looked up at him and said softly, "You and I?"

Her eyes seemed to be melting into his, and Jerry suddenly realized he couldn't handle it. Certainly not on a dishonest level like this. He abruptly pushed away from the wall. "Look, I'm not being honest with you. I've made some changes in myself recently, but . . . but trying to use people is one thing I don't want to learn, even—" He looked at her . . . utterly beautiful, utterly desirable. He remembered the gesture of the coffee cup, and he knew enough about good china to know she had helped him smash a set at least fifty years old. He blurted out the rest of it. "—even if you are what people say you are. Which I'm beginning to doubt very much."

Then he turned quickly and left, brushing past Randolph into the house. Helena watched him until he was out of sight, then she turned thoughtfully toward the steps leading to the garden below.

Questor had retired to the garden after leaving the table. Had he cared to, he could have adjusted his hearing to take in everything Jerry and Lady Helena had said; instead, he had deliberately busied himself cataloging the many varieties of plants and flowers in the garden. He stopped beside the free-form lily pond and stood for a moment, studying his image in the water. He had been outfitted in a white shirt and school tie, a trim black blazer, and gray slacks. Randolph had carried out the white socks and the shoes he had borrowed from the lab lockers, and Questor had not seen them again. Instead, he had been given black socks and comfortable walking shoes of Italian design. Randolph had chosen the wardrobe with an eye toward what looked best on the man . . . one of the reasons he had remained in Lady Helena's employ for ten years. Questor had to admit that the new garments made him look much more like the smartly clad young men he had seen in London. There were many things his tapes had either overlooked or which had been erased.

He heard the crash of the china cup and saucer as Jerry knocked them from the balustrade. An argument? Questor automatically turned up the range of his hearing and heard Lady Helena's light remark about hating that particular pattern. The crash of the second cup and saucer followed. They did not seem to be quarreling, and Questor thought smashing china was a most peculiar manner of expressing affection. However, he had complete faith in Jerry's ability to accomplish his mission.

Questor puzzled over that for a moment. He had begun with a need for Jerry Robinson to fill the enormous gaps in the programmed tapes. As Questor assimilated, sorted, and cataloged various new inputs, he found his reliance on Jerry had become confidence in the young engineer. "My friend Jerry." Those words had been a tremendous revelation to Questor. He knew the dictionary meaning:

friend, one attached to another by esteem, respect, and affection. These were *feelings* that could be given to another. Jerry had given them to him, without reservation or question.

Suddenly he turned. Human ears would not have heard the very faint sound, but Questor had. Lady Helena had stirred some gravel underfoot as she approached from behind him. She paused on the walk, studying him gravely. Finally she took a deep breath and came to his side.

"Mr. Questor," she said in greeting.

He nodded slightly. "You have an interesting variety of decorative flora, madam."

"My husband was very proud of his garden. I've had it kept as he liked it."

"My data does not . . . I mean to say, I did not know you were married."

She smiled briefly, a sad expression flitting across her lips. "I'm a widow, Mr. Questor. Lord Trimble died ten years ago of a heart attack." She paused, then went on softly. "I was very much in love with him."

"I am sorry you were deprived of his presence and his affection. I am sure it was a great loss."

"Yes." She looked at him levelly. "Can you explain why you left Mr. Robinson with me?"

Questor began to move slowly down the path, hands clasped behind his back in imitation of some image his data banks had given him. Lady Helena moved beside him, watching him closely.

"Well?"

Questor saw no reason why he should not respond honestly. Certainly Jerry had accomplished his mission by now. "To secure information by making love to you. I trust you told him what you know of Vaslovik."

Lady Helena stopped, her mouth open in an unladylike gape. Then she brought herself back into control and found her voice. "Mr. Questor, are you trying to be funny?"

"Humor is a quality which seems to elude me."

She raised her eyebrows. *That* was an understatement— possibly the leading contender for understatement of the decade. She folded her arms and calmly resumed the walk along the white gravel path of the garden. "So this is what your friend could not be dishonest about," she said, leading him.

Questor tilted his head to the right, puzzled. "He did not make love to you?"

She cleared her throat, faintly embarrassed. "Nor did he receive any information." She glanced at him and decided to venture the next question as coolly as the female of the species was able. "Is it now your intention to begin where he left off?"

"If vital to an information exchange, I am fully functional. Is it required?"

Lady Helena stopped for the second time in the space of a few minutes—startled, puzzled, and intrigued by this man. He met her eyes with his own direct, bright stare; and she found herself demurely looking away. "I . . . I don't believe I've ever had quite so much trouble knowing how to respond to a question."

"I have merely answered your queries as factually as possible."

She lifted her eyes and studied him for a long moment. She believed him completely . . . as she believed Jerry Robinson. But this man was not Jerry. This Questor was different in some strange and utterly fascinating way which she did not understand nor want to resist. "Perhaps I've forgotten how to deal with honest men," she said finally. She leaned forward slightly, provocatively. "Suppose I were to admit I knew this Vaslovik of yours?"

"I would be gratified."

Lady Helena felt her mouth falling open again and snapped it shut, annoyed. But the man was so obviously leveling with her, she fought down her irritation. Still, some of her annoyance showed in her voice. "You would be gratified? That would be the sum of it?"

"What was Vaslovik's payment for the information you provided him?"

She was too startled to answer for an instant, then she said, "I would prefer to hear *your* best offer, Mr. Questor."

Questor tilted his head to the right, considering it very

carefully. Then he brought his gaze back to rest on her, and she noticed that his usually unreadable eyes had softened. "I have a . . . commodity which I did not know until recently that I could offer." He held out his hand to her formally. "Will you accept my friendship?"

Lady Helena felt her heart jerk and begin to pound so wildly that she was positive they would hear it in the house. She could not speak around the lump that had climbed into her throat, so she simply put her hand in Questor's. His touch was gentle and firm as he politely shook hands with her—and she wondered why she wanted to cry.

Some people said Scotland Yard never closed, never slept, never ceased to function for even a moment. Walter Phillips, Darro's aide, was ready to believe it. Unlike Darro, he had never been able to sleep on planes; and by now, the time difference, jet lag, and plain lack of sleep had begun to catch up to him. He slumped in a chair, watching a police artist finishing a quite accurate sketch of Questor, as identified by the two stewardesses and the immigration official from the airport. Darro was prodding their memories further.

The immigration man studied the sketch closely. "It's getting close now, I'd say, sir. His hair may have been darker. . . ."

"No," Lydia Parker said. "If anything, just a bit lighter." The other girl nodded in agreement.

Darro turned to the artist. "Lighter. I'll trust the female eye on that."

A Scotland Yard inspector entered the room and came to Darro's side. Darro glanced at him questioningly. The inspector extended a paper. "Since you asked to see anything at all unusual, sir, here's a report from a Soho district club. A rather remarkable run of luck."

Darro snatched the paper from the man's hand and examined it. "That's not an extraordinary run of luck, Inspector. That's an android using his computer at full capacity. Get me the people who saw him in there."

"Mr. Darro, you're talking about twenty or more people, some of whom would certainly not come forward."

Darro turned on him, his big frame somehow menacing. "Inspector, I do not care how you do it . . . who you have to talk to, cajole, connive, or otherwise convince anyone who saw the android to come in here. But they are to be here in one hour flat. Is that understood?"

The inspector pulled his mouth in a grimace of distaste, but he nodded. "Yes, sir, I do. I can't say I understand why you're so upset about this robot, though."

"If you had ever met this *android,* Inspector, you would. Believe me . . . you would."

11

Jerry Robinson was only faintly aware of a knock at the door of the room. He sighed and curled a little deeper into the comfortable couch. He had almost made it back into the dream he had been enjoying when a hand tapped his shoulder gently.

"Mr. Robinson," said Randolph. "Sir?"

Jerry shook off the butler's hand, but Randolph did not give up easily. "Mr. *Robinson.*"

Jerry finally managed to pry open his eyes and look around, disoriented, momentarily confused by his surroundings. He heard Randolph's voice asking him some question, but he ignored it for the moment. He was fully dressed, except for the suit jacket, which he had pulled over himself as a blanket. He remembered returning to the guest suite after he had left Lady Helena and waiting there for Questor. He must have fallen asleep on the couch.

"Will you take breakfast here or on the terrace, sir?" Randolph asked patiently for the third time.

Jerry realized that Questor was not in the sitting room area, nor did he seem to be in the bedrooms. Questor didn't sleep; but, until now, he had always told Jerry where he would be. Jerry jumped up, pushing past Randolph, and looked into the adjoining bedroom. "Questor?"

"Mr. Robinson—" Randolph began again.

Jerry whirled back to him anxiously. "Have you seen Questor around?"

"Not this morning, sir."

"Last night?"

Randolph nodded slightly. "Mr. Questor was in Lady Helena's suite when I retired, sir."

"In *her* *suite?* Is she still there? Alone, I mean?"

The butler gave him a very cool, disapproving look. "I really have no intention of inquiring, sir."

Jerry grabbed up his suit jacket and bolted for the door. Randolph shook his head and sighed. Pity these Americans always seemed to take everything so personally. If Mr. Questor had not returned to the guest suite for the night, that was Mr. Questor's business, not Mr. Robinson's. But Randolph supposed he should go along to explain to Lady Helena. She did not appreciate being awakened so early unless it was a matter of importance.

Jerry careened down the curving staircase and along a many-windowed corridor that looked out on the garden. Helena had mentioned in passing that her suite was in the west wing on the ground floor because she liked being near the garden. He found the door and knocked agitatedly. There was no immediate response, and he stopped to shrug into the jacket before he rapped on the door again.

"Lady Helena!" He knocked louder. "Helena, it's Jerry Robinson. Please, it's important."

Mueller's cold, quiet voice interrupted him. "I shall ask this only once, sir. Leave that door immediately."

Jerry started to turn angrily. "No!" His defiance vanished like a drop of water on a hot griddle as he saw Mueller reach toward that ominous bulge inside his jacket. "Oh now, look . . ." Jerry said placatingly. He stumbled through a smile, a shrug, and an attempt to make Mueller see reason. "I'm worried about my friend . . . and your mistress . . . and I can't explain why to you!"

Randolph hurried toward them; but Jerry knew the elderly servant would be no match against the powerful Mueller, even if Randolph was of a mind to interfere. Mueller grabbed Jerry's arm and started to twist it behind his back.

Lady Helena's door opened, and she stepped partway out. All three men stopped, staring at her, as if frozen by her appearance. Her dark hair was down, curling loosely and attractively around her shoulders. Even without make-up, she glowed with a natural beauty—a beauty enhanced by the sheer pink negligee she wore.

Randolph moved first, stepping forward apologetically. "I'm sorry, Lady Helena, but this person—"

"I know what he wants," she interrupted. "Please see to the breakfast arrangements, Randolph."

The butler hesitated, then bowed, and started to back away. "Yes, madam."

Her dark eyes moved to Mueller, who was still holding Jerry's arm in a viselike grip. "I'll speak to you later, Mueller."

Mueller reluctantly released Jerry. He did not like the order, but his instinct was to obey Lady Helena instantly and without question. He nodded to her and left.

Now it was Robinson's turn to come under the scrutiny of those lovely dark eyes. Under other circumstances, he might have enjoyed that searching look; but at the moment he was embarrassed and unsure as to how to proceed.

"You said it was important, Mr. Robinson." Her tone softened. "Jerry?"

"I just . . . wanted to know if you were all right."

Helena smiled faintly. "I've never felt better."

Jerry hesitated; he felt like a small boy, and he didn't like it. Then he realized that she was waiting for him to go on. "I wondered if you knew where my friend might be."

She smiled again. "I do." She opened the door slightly. "Would you like to speak with him?"

Jerry eyed the door, then nodded grimly. "Yes, I think I'll have quite a bit to say to him." He started to push inside the room, but Lady Helena caught and held it, stopping him.

"If you'll wait just a few moments, I'll get dressed and take you to him."

Jerry backed off, mortified over what he had simply and unquestioningly assumed. "He's not . . . ?" She shook her head, slightly amused by the blush that was beginning to crawl up his throat and into his face. "Look, I'm sorry," he began weakly.

Helena smiled again, with just a touch of wry sadness at the edges of her mouth. "So am I."

The Scotland Yard office Darro had appropriated on his arrival had changed only in the personnel who rotated through it during the entire night. Phillips had managed to grab an hour's sleep and five minutes to shave. Darro had not taken any time out at all. Occasionally, Phillips wondered if Vaslovik had made a prototype model of the android and named it Darro. At the moment, the Project Questor chief was questioning a sleepy and rumpled croupier at a private club where two Americans had had "an unusual run of luck." A British security man and a bobby stood unobtrusively in the background as Phillips exhibited the artist's rendering of Questor. The croupier looked at it closely, then glanced up at the security man and Darro. He shrugged and shook his head doubtfully.

"Must be a hundred people roll dice at my table every evening, guv'nor."

"But not many who win close to two thousand pounds in six rolls."

"Yeah, that's a bit unusual, but when it happens, guv'nor, you don't look at the face. You look at the dice." He gestured at the portrait of Questor. "Any kind of reward for him?"

The security man leaned forward. "Twenty pounds."

The croupier looked at the picture again. "Twenty? No, can't say I've ever seen him."

A uniformed London Police supervisor entered quietly with another man. Darro looked around inquiringly. "Supervisor Perkins, sir." The supervisor jerked a thumb at the other man. "He was the casino doorman on duty after midnight that night."

Darro nodded. "Thank you. Please close down that establishment." He waved a hand toward the croupier. "And put this man in jail."

The croupier started up out of his chair, strangling out a protest, but the security man pushed him back into the seat. The supervisor did not change expression.

"On what charges, sir?"

Darro turned to Phillips. "And you're to find another prisoner there who is willing to break both his legs for twenty pounds."

Phillips rose and started for the door. "Yes, sir."

That was too much, even for the supervisor. "Now, just a moment . . ."

Darro did not bother to look up at him. His voice coldly interrupted, "Your instructions from the home secretary's office, Supervisor Perkins?"

"To cooperate in every way, sir, but—"

"Then please do so," Darro said curtly.

The supervisor hesitated. He had been given specific orders to do anything and everything this man Darro wanted. It had been stressed that it was not merely a matter of "hands across the sea," but a problem of such dimension that it could affect the entire country. He squared his shoulders and turned to the bobby. "Take him in."

The croupier bounced to his feet and was grabbed by the burly policeman. "Now just a bloody minute," he howled. "This is *England!*" The bobby ignored his struggles and handcuffed him, then began hauling him toward the door. "Can't nobody take a joke these days? That's the one who came in that night . . . that one there in the picture you got."

"And this man?" Darro held out a photograph of Jerry.

"Yeah . . . yeah, him, too. They were together."

Darro turned to the very impressed and slightly nervous doorman. "Perhaps you'll be as helpful." He showed him the drawing of Questor and the picture of Jerry. "Did you see these men come out of the casino that night?"

The doorman examined the two likenesses and nodded quickly. "Yes, sir! I waved in a taxi for this man and his friend." He tapped the photo of Jerry. "I'm afraid I didn't get the cab number, sir, but—"

Darro cut him off, addressing the supervisor, Perkins. "I want copies of that sketch and the photo in the hands of every London cab driver by noon, Perkins. Have the dispatchers concentrate on the evening-shift drivers."

"By *noon,* sir?" Perkins said, startled.

"I assume you can do it, Perkins, or you would not have been assigned to this case. The home secretary promised me only the top men would be working on it."

"Well . . . I suppose it might be possible, sir."

Darro was already on his feet and heading for the door. Phillips picked up his briefcase and started to follow. Darro did not look around as he went out the door. "I'll check at noon to make sure the dispatchers have enough to cover all shifts, Perkins."

"Ah, yes sir," the supervisor said. He was beginning to believe it could be done. In fact, he decided, it definitely could be done. Which was what Darro had known from the beginning.

Jerry followed Lady Helena down steep flights of steps through two subbasements before they reached the level which had been the original cellar. Jerry had had time to notice that she had not bothered with makeup but had merely tied her hair back with a pale blue scarf and slipped into a dark blue suede pantsuit. As they threaded their way back into the depths of a well-stocked wine cellar, Jerry reflected that Lady Helena was probably one of the few women of the world who would wear a designer outfit into a murky, dusty basement. She stopped at a wall completely covered by wine racks holding bottles of vintage years from every major European winery.

"Watch carefully which bottles I adjust," she said. Very skillfully, not disturbing any dust, she pulled three bottles an inch out of their horizontal resting places.

"Here . . . here . . . wait five seconds . . ." She counted them off silently, and then she moved the third bottle. ". . . then here."

She stepped back, glancing toward a section of the wall. Jerry could hear a faint motor hum, then a whole section of the wall wine rack hinged out, turning to reveal a dark recess beyond. Helena gestured at the wine bottle "combination" again.

"Memorize that. If the bottles are not pulled in that exact sequence, that concrete wall will slide down to hide this passage." She looked at Jerry levelly. "Your friend assured me I can trust you."

Jerry stepped partway into the dark recess and nervously looked up at the tons of concrete poised overhead. "Just . . . step under a hundred tons of concrete . . . and what?"

She reached out to touch his arm lightly. "Jerry . . . trust me. As you should have last night."

"Questor told you you could trust me?"

"Yes."

"He doesn't . . . he *can't* lie about things like that." They exchanged a look—one of understanding and mutual respect. Jerry stepped into the recess. Lady Helena pushed the three bottles back into their original positions in reverse order. The motor hum was heard again, and the wine rack partition swung closed. Jerry was left standing in utter darkness . . . waiting.

12

It seemed like the silent darkness went on for an hour, but Jerry realized it was probably only a few minutes. Suddenly an intense white light flashed onto him, instantly adjusting upward to center on his face and reveal his features. Questor's familiar voice boomed over an intercom system.

"Yes, my friend, Jerry. Please enter."

A panel in front of Jerry slid up, and he stepped out of the recess into an octagonal room of dark translucent glass. Jerry caught his breath as he looked around. As an engineer, he could appreciate the complexity of the hardware . . . and he could also appreciate the fact that the technology in the room was far beyond the abilities of any country he knew. On sections of the dark glass, rectangles of information readouts appeared—various important activities taking place around the world, scientific information, digital readouts, stock market quotations, views of earth from satellites. In the exact center, Questor was seated inside a circular control-panel station. Directly over his head, a concave dome glowed, pulsating, as if myriad data were being beamed from it directly into him. It was remarkably like a more advanced and sophisticated version of the input dome in the Project Questor lab.

Jerry moved quietly to where Questor's fingers strayed across the control-panel buttons. The android depressed several keys in rapid succession, and several of the readout rectangles on the wall faded to black. Then other information began to appear in the same places. Jerry stared at it in awe. It was like a giant organ keyboard on

which events and information from the whole world could
be played.

"Questor! What is this place?"

The android was concentrating almost totally on the
information he was absorbing and analyzing. He did not
look at Jerry and flicked him only a fraction of his attention. "One moment, please." He touched another control
and looked toward a portion of the translucent wall.
Jerry followed his look.

The rectangle flashed on. Images of boats and other
watercraft appeared at an incredible rate of speed—hun-
dreds per minute. Most were unfamiliar to Jerry as the
series of pictures began. They were ships from ancient
cultures—small, large, commercial, military, pleasure
craft. As the designs proceeded down the centuries toward more modern ships, Jerry began to recognize some
of the flashing images—sailing ships, submarines, war-
ships, tugs, freighters, tankers, passenger liners.

An electronic sound hummed softly from the control
panel, and pinpoints of light from overhead flickered on
Questor's face. He shut off the images of boats and concentrated on information obviously being beamed to him
from the dome above. That shut off automatically, and
Questor finally turned to Jerry.

"In answer to your question, this was Vaslovik's information center. Judging from this laser-telemetry device"—
he waved at the overhead dome—"it seems to have been
designed to be used by me. Although for what ultimate
purpose, I am still unclear."

"It's exactly that purpose which frightens me, Questor!
Do you understand what all this implies?" He pointed at
one of the picture rectangles on the wall. "That's the
Congress of the United States in session there." He
pointed to another. "And there—that has to be a part of
the Soviet Defense Command . . . and Lord knows what
those weapons systems and digital readouts mean."

Questor had turned away to begin keying the control
panel again, but Jerry reached in angrily and pushed the
android's hand away from the board. "The boats I understand. You're looking for Vaslovik. But the rest of

this . . ." He shook his head, attempting to find the words to make Questor realize the enormity of the situation. "Questor, try to understand the implications of this. Suppose Vaslovik isn't a good man. Suppose he isn't even sane!"

"One's creator not sane?" He turned to Jerry, his head tilted thoughtfully. "An interesting question. How would you answer that query in your own case, Jerry?"

Jerry's eye caught a glimpse of another image which had flickered on. He turned to look at it fully, startled and shocked. A distinguished gentleman sat on the edge of a bed in the early stages of what he apparently hoped would be the seduction of a lovely young woman. The young woman also hoped for the same, if her help in easing off the man's jacket and shirt was correctly interpreted.

"That's somebody's *bedroom!*"

Questor nodded expressionlessly, reached out, and touched a control key. The image of the two people grew larger and more intimate. Questor eyed it clinically. "This incident will affect a surplus grain trade agreement tomorrow, which will, in turn, affect the death toll in a famine which will occur soon in Bangladesh unless certain antifungicide studies at the University of Mexico are completed and disseminated in time." He indicated another rectangle which flashed out a series of equations and computations. "On the other hand, a current plague outbreak in Malaysia may become epidemic resulting in a sufficient . . . death toll to create a rice surplus which could be shipped to the famine area. An interesting problem, since it appears several hundred thousand humans will die one way or the other."

"*What are you talking about?*"

Questor looked at Jerry, mildly surprised. "Vaslovik, of course. Certain developments in either the grain fungicide or plague situation would indicate his presence at that point and I would concentrate my search in that area. Concurrently, I am seeking indications of his other areas of knowledge or interest in other parts of the world.

Meanwhile, the inefficient verbalizing to you of these simple processes is delaying that search somewhat."

Jerry slammed down his fist atop the control panel. *Why* wouldn't Questor see? He pulled himself together and held out his hands in an almost pleading gesture. "Questor, I *must* know why Vaslovik built this place! Do you understand what information like this can be sold for? How it can be used? Do you know how Lady Helena makes use of this information?"

"I have not inquired," Questor said quietly. "However, I have learned something of her background."

"How?" Jerry asked suspiciously.

"From these records, of course." Questor pointed toward a rectangle which began to flash up images of a skinny, wide-eyed teenager who bore a faint resemblance to Lady Helena. "Vaslovik found her in Yorkshire as a fourteen-year-old. He taught her to become what she is —poised, charming, sophisticated. He made her wealthy."

"Pygmalion," Jerry muttered wryly.

"You refer to the Greek myth of Galatea and the King of Cyprus?"

"Do you have a reference to George Bernard Shaw?"

Questor tilted his head slightly to the right, apparently running some data through his information banks. Then he looked at Jerry. "Ah, yes, I see the connection in the literary sense. However, there is no indication Vaslovik fell in love with his creation. Helena met Lord Trimble when she was twenty-one. He was forty. They were married three months later and had a very happy marriage until Lord Trimble's death some six years later. Vaslovik was a frequent house guest, and there is every indication that Lord Trimble was at least aware of this information center and his wife's activities."

"And he didn't interfere?"

"It would seem not. Lady Trimble continued to move among the top financial, political, and social circles of the world. Through an organization she put together under Vaslovik's supervision, she gathers information . . . of all kinds . . . and for years has had it passed on to Vaslovik."

Jerry's heart sank. Helena had asked him to trust her. "She's a spy?"

"A clearing house of information, covering a strangely catholic group of areas. Gossip, scandal, political developments, military preparations. This room reflects that information." Questor turned back to the control panel and became lost again in the information input and computations as the pinpoints of laser telemetry increased from the overhead dome.

Jerry watched him, concern growing in him like a cancer. His fears about Vaslovik and Questor had forced him close to a decision, but there was one question he still had to ask. "Questor, if Darro's checking everything, and I think he will be, won't he get a report of unusual radio-wave concentration in this area?"

"This system does not employ radio-wave transmission as you understand it, my friend. We are quite safe here." Questor did not look around again. He was absorbed in seeking, rejecting, analyzing information.

Jerry turned away. There was no place to sit down— no place for anyone in this room, except Questor. Jerry moved back toward the entrance and made his way out of the information center.

Lady Helena was already seated at the breakfast table on the terrace. There were places for two. As soon as Jerry appeared in the doorway, Helena poured a fresh cup of coffee and added cream and sugar exactly the way he had had it the night before. She handed him the cup and saucer as he sat down opposite her.

"Randolph will have your bacon and eggs in a moment," she said.

"How did he know what I would have asked for?"

She smiled gently. "Mr. Questor left instructions—"

"For the care and feeding of one engineer, male, human, 1945 model," Jerry concluded sourly.

"If the food isn't satisfactory, you can ask for something else, Jerry. My kitchen pantry can stand the strain."

"It's not that, Helena. *I'm* not a project he can program—"

Questor's voice behind him startled him. The android had approached without a sound. "You are most adept at understatement, my friend Jerry. But you are right. You are not . . . a project."

He settled in a chair between them as Helena leaned forward, all business. "Your passports will be here by tomorrow morning. The other matter you mentioned is being arranged."

"What's this about passports?"

Questor tilted his head to the right and regarded Jerry curiously. "You insist they are necessary. I have persuaded Lady Helena to provide us with the essential documentation."

"Forgeries?"

Helena smiled cheerfully. "Prove it if you can."

Jerry decided not to try to answer. Instead, he dug into the plate of scrambled eggs and bacon Randolph discreetly set before him. Questor handed Lady Helena a thick file of papers.

"I think you will find no difficulty in executing these. One further thing—I have in my mind an extremely indistinct image of an aquatic vehicle; would such a thing relate in any way to Vaslovik?"

"Not that I know of," Helena said. "He showed no interest in sailing. In the last few years I knew him, in fact, he showed little interest in anything except some project he wouldn't talk about. The poor man . . . he was failing right before my eyes."

"When did you last see him?" Jerry asked quickly.

"Three years ago," Helena said. She looked away sadly. "I've missed him."

Jerry realized that Helena meant it, and he decided to skirt that subject for the moment. But there was something else. He turned to Questor, frowning. "What 'other matter' did you have arranged?"

"A private jet," Questor said calmly.

"A private . . . *jet?*"

"It seemed most expeditious."

"Oh, I'm sure. But chartering one of those things must cost a fortune."

Questor nodded. "Perhaps. But I did not charter it. I bought it."

"I suppose that was most expeditious, too."

"Yes. Do not concern yourself as to the cost. The money Mr. Campbell's office is investing on our behalf is a continuing process. Most convenient."

Helena stood up abruptly, excusing herself. She had begun to sense Jerry's feelings of concern and agitation and decided to let the two talk it out between themselves. Jerry waited until she was out of earshot, then turned back to Questor. "You said Campbell is investing the money on *our* behalf. . . ."

"That is correct. Had you not given me the money to make the initial gambling venture, we would not have had money to invest in stocks and bonds which are now accruing both profit and interest. Half the proceeds are in your name." He studied Jerry's face and frowned slightly. "You are troubled, my friend Jerry. Why?"

"Sometimes it's very hard to know the right course to take."

Questor leaned back in his chair with an expression that could almost be interpreted as relief. "I see. I am gratified to learn this. I feared the phenomenon was peculiar to myself."

"But you still intend to use that information down there? You still intend to follow your programmed imperative?"

"I had thought that point was clear. I must. Something in here"—Questor tapped his chest—"tells me I must find Vaslovik."

"No matter what?"

Questor hesitated, thinking it over. Then he looked up at Jerry with those bright, clear, candid eyes. "Yes. Nothing must prevent me from accomplishing that mission."

Jerry sat for a long time in the sitting room of the guest suite, staring at the phone on the desk. He had been over and over every moment since the afternoon when Questor had been activated. Knowing what he did about the information center in the subbasement, knowing Questor would not stop nor be stopped until he accomplished whatever it was Vaslovik had programmed him to do, Jerry had only one choice. He choked back a wave of regret and went to the phone to dial the long distance operator.

The operator came on the line, and Jerry found it hard to talk around the lump in his throat. "Operator, this is a person-to-person call to Mr. Geoffrey B. Darro. You may reach him through . . . through the metropolitan police in London. If not, I have a number in California."

13

Jerry Robinson was quite drunk. At least, he should have been. By his own vague count, he was on his twelfth Wild Turkey bourbon and branch water; but he merely felt depressed and moderately inebriated as he chased worried thoughts around his head. Randolph set a fresh drink before him on the terrace table and removed two empty glasses.

Helena stepped out onto the terrace and paused, puzzled, when she saw Jerry slumped in one of the lounge chairs, staring glassy-eyed out at the garden. "Randolph." The butler stopped on his way past her. "How long has he been at that?"

"Since early this afternoon, madam." Randolph looked around at Jerry and lowered his voice. "I tried to lighten the drinks, but he asked for the bottle of bourbon himself and he's been adding it to the drinks I bring him." He shook his head. "Extraordinary."

"Why do you say that?"

"Madam, the amount of liquor he has consumed in just two hours would flatten an African elephant. But he keeps telling me to bring him another."

"I'll see to it, Randolph. Thank you."

Jerry watched her approach through half-squinted eyes, and raised his glass to her in greeting. "Ah . . . Helena. 'How sweet and lovely dost thou make the shame which, like a canker in the fragrant rose . . . doth spot the beauty of thy . . . of thy budding name. Oh, in what sweets dost thou thy sins enclose. That . . . that tongue that tells the story of thy days, making las-lascivious comments on thy sport, cannot dispraise but in a kind of praise; naming thy name blesses an ill report. Oh, what a mansion have those vices got which for their habitation chose out thee, where beauty's veil doth cover every blot, and all things turn to fair that eyes can see. . . . Take heed, dear heart, of this large privilege; the hardest knife ill-used doth lose his edge. . . .' "

"Bravo, Jerry," Helena said as she sat down beside him. "Randolph was right. You are quite extraordinary."

"Howzzat?"

"Anyone who can go through a bottle of bourbon and still recite one of Shakespeare's sonnets is rather remarkable."

Jerry contemplated the bottle and the drink on the table and nodded solemnly. "I'm a closet inaluctual."

"Intellectual?"

"That's what I said."

Helena smiled slightly, amused. "Jerry, what is it? I suppose Emil's information center must have been a surprise to you."

Jerry looked over at her and wagged a finger in her direction. "I'm more interested in why you decided to show that room to Questor."

"Partly intuition, I suppose." She glanced at him almost demurely. "I suppose you know Mr. Questor is a most unusual man."

"I'll drink to *that*," Jerry said promptly. He took a hefty swig of the fresh drink Randolph had brought, then reached for the bottle of bourbon and added another two fingers of the liquor. "Why do *you* think Questor is . . . uh . . . unusual?"

"One gets the feeling he's almost incapable of dishonesty. And then there's his way of speaking. The words he uses. They reminded me so much of Emil, I realized they had to have been very, very close."

"And I'll drink to *that!*" He downed another healthy swallow.

Helena frowned and reached out a hand to touch his arm gently. "Jerry, what's troubling you? Questor did explain about what we do here?"

"I can see what you do here." He waved the glass

around, taking in the house and grounds. Some of the liquor slopped over the rim of the glass, but Jerry ignored it. "And *how* you do here. Very, very well!"

Randolph had returned with another drink on a tray and hovered in the background, not intruding on the conversation. Jerry paused to take another drink, and Randolph stepped forward to set down the fresh glass. Helena waved him back.

"Mr. Robinson is going to have a large pot of black coffee, Randolph. . . . and the surprise of his life."

Jerry sat up straight, supported by injured dignity. "I refuse to sober up."

Helena's lovely face set in grim, unyielding lines. "Mr. Robinson, you are not going to have a choice."

Questor still sat in the circular console in the information center, deep in concentration on the data flooding into him. The look on his face had changed—a touch of sadness. If he could feel, it might have been despair. He stirred, slowly reached out to the control board, and began shutting down the equipment. The readouts began to fade, one by one. The laser telemetry lessened in quantity and intensity until it was gone, leaving him seated in darkness except for a pool of light around the circular console. Questor tapped one more key.

"This message tape is to be delivered to Mr. Robinson." He swiveled around in the chair slightly and saw himself reflected in one of the wall rectangles, as if on camera. The message would be a videotape, and he spoke directly to Jerry. "My friend . . . I regret we shall never meet again. Until now, my programming has prevented me from informing you that my creator designed within me a time limit in which to find him." He glanced around at the banks of equipment, the blank dark walls. "I now conclude further search is useless. There is no trace of my creator. There has been none for three years. In seven days, my friend Jerry, I will cease to exist. I must now leave to prepare myself for that event. You must consider me merely a device which has failed its programmed function. I . . . wish I had learned more of man . . . of your own concept of your creator. I have much to criticize in man, but I believe there is even more to admire. Had I more time, I might have even learned to understand man's greatest of all achievements . . . his ability to feel love for his fellows. But I thank you for teaching me the meaning, at least, of the word *friendship*."

He reached out and depressed the key again. The rectangle on the wall melted away to blackness.

Helena poured Jerry another cup of coffee, which he dutifully drank without pausing for breath. He looked a little less disheveled, though his shirt collar was unbuttoned and his tie had disappeared. He set down the cup of coffee, which she instantly refilled.

"I *want* to believe you, Helena," Jerry said. "But there's equipment here that can tap into any place in the world! Without being detected. It makes the CIA look like amateurs."

"Jerry . . . isn't the important question *how* we use it?"

"It's too much power for one man to have. Even a genius!"

Helena leaned forward earnestly, trying to explain. It wasn't the kind of thing that worked out logically if it was put down on paper. It was idealistic . . . perhaps too much so for a world grown increasingly cynical. The concept appeared at least once each generation . . . somewhere, someone voiced it. It wasn't always heard . . . seldom accepted. And yet it was so simple.

"Jerry, Emil Vaslovik wasn't just a *genius*. He must have been the kindest, most decent man who ever lived. He built what you saw here so his knowledge could be used to *help* people. Don't you understand? Our world is fragmented by national jealousies, greed, religious and ideological conflicts. There is no *one* place on earth where someone can look past a border to see what is needed there, and past another border to see what is there that can help."

"The Bangladesh famine and the fungicide studies in Mexico."

Helena smiled quickly, "Yes, exactly. Emil didn't want

to change the world or control it. All this was worth it if
he could save a life here and there, help a young man
somewhere become the leader or teacher he was meant to
be. . . ."

"How would Vaslovik know some child was meant to
be a leader or a teacher?"

Helena paused. "Well, perhaps not a child, but a stu-
dent who showed great promise and ability. Poverty kills
so many of them. Lack of education defeats others.
Emil's way helped them grow and learn and contribute."

Jerry pushed to his feet, agitated, confused. What he'd
heard sat uneasily in him, especially after what he'd done.
Randolph quietly entered as Jerry interrupted Helena.
"Excuse me, Helena," Jerry said. "I've got to get to Questor."

"Sir, Mr. Questor's gone," Randolph said. He turned
to Helena. "He asked me to thank you for your kindness,
madam."

"Gone where?" Jerry moved to Randolph anxiously.
"Did he say anything?"

"He left a message for you in the information center,
sir. I did hear him ask Sebastian to drive him to the village."

"Helena, I'll need to borrow a car."

She frowned, confused and concerned. "Do you think
it's wise, Jerry? Mr. Questor must know what he's doing."

"That's what I'm afraid of." He ran inside, heading for
the information center, calling over his shoulder as he
went. "Have that car ready when I get back upstairs!"

The caravan of police and military vehicles careened
down the road so wildly that oncoming drivers pulled
over to the side to let them by. Every man in the group
was loaded with weapons and ammunition. Overhead, two
helicopters fluttered into view, coming from the direction
of Trimble Manor.

Darro sat in the back of a police sedan with the police
supervisor. The voice of one of the helicopter pilots
crackled through a radio telephone, underscored by the

roar of the chopper engine and the steady hum of the blades.

"Holding at three thousand feet, sir. Robinson has just left the manor house also and is driving east toward the village."

Darro flicked down the "talk" button on his microphone. "Keep him in sight. We're having all exits from the village cut off. If Questor and Robinson are there, we've got them."

Questor had come to like the quiet oases of green trees, flowers, and lawns which humans called parks. He stood quietly under a tree, watching a platoon of children attacking the slides and swings and seesaws of the play area. The weather was warm, and a faint breeze barely riffled the leaves into a swaying dance. Someone skilled in topiary art had shaped a number of trees and shrubs into fanciful animal shapes . . . elephants, giraffes, horses, bears, and seals balancing balls on their noses. One of the children had draped bright pink and yellow crepe streamers around the necks of several of the greenery animals, giving them a pert, carnival look.

The limousine and chauffeur waited on the street, but Questor could not bring himself to leave immediately. He had purchased a small bag of birdseed and stood idly tossing it out to the daintily pecking flock of sparrows that hopped about at his feet. "All creatures great and small . . ." There were so many he would like to have seen for himself—and people—and places.

Jerry Robinson wheeled along the street in an open MG and pulled over to park when he saw the limousine. He shut off the ignition and scrambled out of the car, running across the grass toward Questor. The android did not turn around as Jerry came up beside him. Instead, he shook the last crumbs of birdseed out of the paper bag.

"Questor! That message you left—"

"A curious world, Jerry. Squalor, ugliness, greed, struggle—and yet, so much beauty here, so many persons to hope man survives."

Jerry impatiently brushed aside Questor's calm philosophy. "I want to know what happens in seven days. What did you mean you'll 'cease to exist'?"

The android shook his head slightly, still gazing off at the topiary garden. "Without my creator, I have no purpose, my friend. He provided me with extinction in that event so I could not be misused."

"Don't be so damned cold about it! You're talking about *dying*."

"Death occurs to living things, Jerry. Do you consider me to be alive?" He brushed past Jerry and moved toward the limousine. Jerry trotted after him and caught his arm to stop him.

"Listen! On that message tape, you mentioned friendship. That means sharing someone's troubles, risking things with him, confiding in him."

"But does it not also mean protecting one's friend? My form of extinction would destroy you."

"Questor, you've *got* to explain what happens to you in seven days!"

Questor hesitated, then leveled his direct, honest eyes at Jerry. He decided it would be better if his friend knew the truth. There was a core of stubborn determination in Jerry that might cause him to put himself in danger if he did not receive an answer. Questor could not allow that. "My fusion furnace will overload, Jerry. I will become a nuclear bomb."

"*What?*" Jerry stared at him, stunned. Then he pulled himself together. There *must* be alternatives. "Look, I can change the furnace, divert the overload. . . ."

"Only my creator can alter that," Questor said calmly. "I must remove myself far from all life. I must not endanger others when I expire." Questor moved toward the limousine again. "That must include you, my friend Jerry."

"Questor . . ."

"You will stay here. No one will blame you for any of my actions. I have left evidence to prove your innocence." He nodded to the chauffeur, who opened the car door for him. Jerry grabbed Questor's arm and swung him around. "Questor!"

"Yes, Jerry?"

Jerry fidgeted guiltily. It was difficult to say what he had to, but he found the nerve to blurt it out. "I called Darro. I told him you were at Trimble Manor. I'm sorry. . . ."

Questor nodded, understanding, and waved Jerry into the back seat of the limousine. Jerry got in, followed by the android. Before the chauffeur could shut the door, a police lorry rolled into view, blocking the village street ahead of them. Uniformed police began to boil out of it. Jerry whirled, looking behind them. Armed British troops and more uniformed policemen pulled up to block other streets. Questor started to get out of the car, but Jerry pulled him back.

"No, don't try it. I'll talk to Darro, explain—"

"I have no choice but to attempt escape. I must remove myself to some distant area of the world, my friend."

"Don't keep calling me that! I'm the one who gave you away!"

"Then you must have believed it necessary for some good reason. Does that make you less my friend?"

Jerry stared at him and found it difficult to try to speak around the painful lump in his throat. He looked away before Questor's bright, honest eyes caught the glitter of tears in his own.

A squad of soldiers armed with rifles and submachine guns was moving in, led by a lieutenant. "Hold it there!" the officer shouted. "Which of you is Questor?"

Jerry spun toward Questor and spoke quickly and quietly. "All right, when I move, go the other way *fast.* Darro promised they wouldn't shoot."

"Yes, I understand."

Jerry braced himself, then opened the door beside him, and shoved it open. He stepped out, hands up, shouting, *"This way, here! I'm the one! I'm Questor!"*

The squad of soldiers moved closer, their guns trained on Jerry. Questor slid out the other side of the car and began to walk away as casually as possible. Behind him, Jerry kept talking, trying to divert the soldiers' attention as long as possible. A policeman cutting across the park blocked Questor's way, drawing his revolver. Questor sprang forward, snatched the pistol from his hands, and flung it away.

A young soldier came around the corner of a parked lorry just in time to see Questor disarm the police officer. The android left the officer and headed straight toward the young soldier. The boy brought his weapon up to firing position.

"Hold your fire!" an officer shouted. Jerry turned at the same moment and saw what was happening. *"Don't shoot!"*

But the young soldier's hands had already tightened on the weapon, and it bucked as he fired a burst directly at Questor. The android stopped, staggered, then began to fall backward. He landed in a crumpled heap, his unwinking eyes staring at the sky.

Jerry ran to him and knelt beside him to prop up his head and shoulders. Questor's eyes seemed to have dulled, and his head rolled limply to the side. Jerry bowed his head over him.

"Questor! Questor, I'm sorry."

The lieutenant in charge of the squad came up beside Jerry and stared down at the android. The submachine gun bullets had ripped the jacket and shirt across the abdominal area, but nothing else was visible. The lieutenant frowned. "No blood. Are you certain he's hit?"

Jerry looked up at him, then down at Questor again. "There's blood. *There's blood all over!"*

14

Jerry reflected glumly that the Project Questor lab and Cal Tech had not changed noticeably in the time they had been away. Then he realized that it had only been five days since Questor had been activated. It felt like a year ... or more.

He glanced at the burly man in the laboratory clean suit beside him as they prepared to enter the lab. Darro had found Questor's evidence, declaring Jerry innocent of any wrongdoing. But Jerry knew that Darro trusted him no more than he trusted any of the scientists who had attempted to steal the Questor secret. They were being tolerated here and now because they were needed.

Darro keyed his identification into the door device, and it slid open to admit him. Jerry did the same. As soon as the automatic door opened, he hurried to the assembly pallet where Questor's body lay.

The android was motionless, his eyes still staring up, unblinking. The submachine gun bullets had ripped vicious holes in the plastiskin. Wires once again ran into the circuits beneath the entry flap in his side. The five scientists stood unhappily beside the pallet and at the monitoring stations.

"Well?" Darro said.

Audret sighed and spoke first. "No brain-case injuries, fortunately. But several main servo-systems are gone, and we fear perhaps even deeper severance of—"

Darro interrupted curtly. "In simple English, please. *Can it be repaired?*"

"*Him,* not 'it,' " Jerry snapped.

120

Dr. Bradley looked up from her monitoring station. "No brain waves at all."

"Clinically dead, if that is the appropriate term," Gorlov said. He glanced from Robinson to Darro. "Without Robinson's assistance, the answer to your question is no."

"Well, Robinson?"

Jerry looked back at Darro coldly. "I've answered that already, Darro. Only on my terms."

"You made your terms when you called me, Robinson."

"That was a mistake. I won't make the same one again."

"I will not bargain!"

Jerry nodded briefly. "Then you just let him lie there another one hundred forty-four hours and see what happens, Darro."

Darro angrily moved a step forward, flinging out one arm to indicate the room, the scientists, the technology concentrated in that one place. "Five of the finest scientists in the world assure me nuclear fusion cannot be triggered to overload."

"Will you bet your life on it, Darro?"

They stood there nose to nose, sizing each other up. Darro weighed the change in Jerry from pleasant, easygoing young engineer to the defiant, confident man who stood before him. But Darro was a gambler, and he knew a bluff when he saw one.

"Bet," he said flatly.

"Call," Jerry shot back. "If you, your five *fine* scientists, and Pasadena are still here six days from now, give me a telephone call. I'll be in Iowa." He turned and started for the door.

Just as it slid open for him, Darro called out, "What are your terms, Robinson?"

Jerry stopped, took a deep breath, and faced Darro again. "The lab under my control, these people obeying my orders, and . . . and if he is not fully functioning within five days, a jet standing by to transport him to a safe nuclear-blast location."

"Agreed," Darro said tightly. "And now, if you're through . . ."

"Not quite," Jerry said. "I'll start work right away, but I want you out of this lab. Now. And I don't want to see you back in here until I give the word."

Darro froze, rage working in his face until it turned a deep red. Then, silently, he left the room.

Dr. Chen expertly ran a heat sealer over the last rip in the plastiskin made by the bullets. He stepped back and examined his work critically. Except for some cosmetology coloration needed at the repair points, Questor's body was as perfect as before. Chen looked across the inert android to Jerry, who worked on the circuits beneath the flap of plastiskin.

"I can reapply necessary coloration later. Do you require other assistance?"

Jerry shook his head wearily. "To do what? What I need now is Vaslovik to explain these components." He waved a hand vaguely. "Why don't you turn in? The others will be back at seven."

"Perhaps if you slept a few hours, Mr. Robinson," Chen suggested.

"Would you?"

Chen studied the engineer. Jerry's face had a two-day beard stubble. His eyes were an interesting shade of pink and had a tendency to water. But his mouth had a stubborn set, and Chen knew no argument of his would sway him. "I understand," he said. "Please call me when I can assist further."

Chen left, and Jerry turned back to Questor's still form. He studied it, then rubbed his eyes to try to ease the stinging behind them. Nothing they had done so far had gotten a response from Questor. Superficial repairs had been made, but Questor had not been reactivated. Jerry spoke half to Questor, half to himself.

"We've got your servos all back in operation. But I'm stuck. The bullets tore open some components no one's ever seen inside—"

He stopped as one of Questor's fingers laboriously tapped twice on the edge of the pallet, as if in a signal. Jerry leaned closer to Questor's ear and spoke into it. "Questor . . . Questor, it's Jerry. Tap twice if you understand."

He waited for the longest moment in his life. Then Questor's finger moved and tapped twice.

Jerry let out a breath with a rush of relief. "Thank God! Questor, listen carefully. There are components damaged I've never seen inside before. Can you answer some yes-or-no questions about them?"

Questor's finger moved again, slowly tapping once, then again.

Jerry closed his eyes and gripped Questor's hand as he would a brother's. A couple of unexpected rivulets of water ran down his cheeks, and he did not know if it was relief or fatigue or just honest tears. And he didn't care.

Darro maintained his own vigil, perhaps more rigorous than Jerry's. He sat at his desk signing a letter, then handed it to his assistant, Phillips. "That'll be all, Phillips," he said. The assistant retired gratefully, and Darro restlessly moved to a small-screen video monitor beside his desk. He snapped it on.

The video monitor lit up with a flickering, pale blue image of the lab. It was empty, except for Jerry, who bent intently over Questor's body, working at something. His voice hollowly came over the monitor's speaker.

"Next, the left abdominal stringer servo. Shall I bypass it now?"

Darro frowned and ran the monitor camera quickly around the lab. There *was* no one else there . . . except the android. His hand flicked another control, and the camera zoomed in to a closer shot of the pallet. It was just in time to see Questor's fingers move, tapping out a yes answer.

Jerry worked carefully, delicately, moving aside circuitry as if it were tissue and muscles. Questor's eyes fluttered and blinked, then focused on his friend. His mouth moved with difficulty, at first barely able to articulate the sounds.

"Je . . . Jer . . ."

Jerry looked up quickly, concerned. "What is it?"

"Jerry . . . you must not . . . fear to . . . probe deeper. I . . . feel no pain. I am . . . not a human patient."

Robinson looked away guiltily. "You're the only one involved in this entire thing who has shown any *human* decency. Including me!"

"Do not blame yourself. I understand."

"Do you, Questor? Then you know more than all the psychologists and psychiatrists and students of mankind since the world began."

"Please . . . go on with your work. It is necessary."

Jerry nodded and began to probe the intricate circuitry and transistor setup inside Questor's body. Suddenly he stopped, and his eyes darted to the android's face. His voice shook slightly as he said, "Questor . . . a sealed covering of the furnace has been pierced."

"Let me . . . investigate it," Questor said.

Jerry quickly adjusted one of the lab cameras so that Questor could see the section on a nearby monitor. He set it on the closest zoom he could. Questor's right hand moved slowly, dipping into the abdominal cavity, probing lightly with his sensitive fingers. He stopped. "Look closely here." Jerry bent forward, scanning the area Questor pointed out—and looked up in sudden alarm. "Do not touch the device, Jerry."

"It was hidden inside the casing. What is it?"

"The nuclear timing device."

"Questor, together, can't we remove the timer?"

Questor shook his head briefly, one slight shake left to right. "Only Vaslovik can remove it without detonation."

Suddenly Darro's voice came over the outside speaker, crackling in on low volume. "Robinson, this is Darro! Tell the machine to play dead until I get there. I want no one else to know it's working again."

Jerry's mouth tightened into a hard line, but he turned

to the two-way speaker and flicked it into a "send" position. "All right, Darro. We'll wait for you."

Darro entered the lab almost cautiously, moving toward Questor's pallet to stare down at the android's body. Questor's eyes were closed, but the steady rise and fall of his chest had been restored. Jerry stood beside the assembly pallet almost protectively. Darro glanced across Questor at him, then down at the android again.

"Hello. My name is Darro."

Questor's eyes snapped open, and he stared at Darro. Finally, he moved his head in an acknowledging nod. "Mr. Robinson has told me you gave orders that I was not to be injured. For that attempt, at least, I thank you."

"But I'm still the one who curtailed your freedom. What do you think of that?"

"What would you think of it?" Jerry snapped.

"Let the android answer, please."

"Each of us has his own life instructions, Mr. Darro. You must, of course, be true to yours."

Darro's eyes narrowed, but his tone of voice did not change. It remained as cold as it always had. "I do not need advice from a machine."

Questor's eyes had not left his. Darro felt faintly uncomfortable under that penetrating stare that seemed to cut through the walls he had built carefully and into the places where he lived alone.

"Or is it, Mr. Darro, that you do not *want* it?"

The corners of Darro's mouth bent up slightly, a cold imitation of a smile. "Or is there a third reason for this interview?"

Questor nodded. "The most likely one. For some reason of your own, it is important to determine if I feel anger or emotion. I do not."

"I envy you for lacking them."

"And I, Mr. Darro, would trade anything to feel . . . to be human."

"Then Vaslovik's machine is a fool." Darro waited for

Questor to respond. When the android did not, the project chief turned to Jerry. "I must talk to you, Mr. Robinson."

Jerry did not like that faint bend of the mouth Darro used for a smile. He flicked a look at Questor, who seemed almost peaceful and at rest. Darro had already turned away and was walking out of the lab, confident that Jerry would follow. Jerry touched Questor's shoulder lightly, and Questor spoke quietly.

"Go with him, Jerry. There is no danger to me for the moment."

Jerry nodded and trailed after Darro.

Darro wasted no time in his office. He went directly to a cabinet beside the lab monitor screen and took out a tiny electronic device. He handed it to Jerry.

Jerry flipped it over in his hands, examining it with a frown. "A radio transmitter?"

"To be placed inside the android's body."

"Are you asking me to betray him a second time, Darro?"

Darro slammed his hand against the cabinet. "Not 'him,' damn you! It is a machine!"

"Either way, Darro, this wasn't part of our agreement."

"I've reneged on that part of it."

Jerry nearly dropped the radio transmitter. "*You? You're* going to renege on a contract? Your whole reputation has been built on the fact that you've never broken your word."

"There's still a private jet standing by, as you requested," Darro said, ignoring Jerry's last statement as if it were a non sequitur. "You've got less than five days to button up the android and try to find Vaslovik."

"With you following our radio signal all the way," Jerry said bitterly.

"The way I see it, Robinson, we all really want the same thing. Vaslovik. Find him—if you can—and all our problems are solved. Or the jet can dump the android on the atoll we've selected. Let it blow itself up." He tapped the transmitter in Jerry's hand. "It's up to you."

15

The townhouse was in the east eighties. Jerry admired it as the limousine drove up and stopped in front of it. He had not been to New York since he had started on Project Questor, and if their mission here had not been so grim, he might have enjoyed being back. He glanced at Questor as the chauffeur got out of the car to open the door for them and see to the bags.

"Lady Helena?" Jerry asked.

"A most efficient woman," Questor said.

Jerry followed him out of the car and up the stairs, wondering about Questor's seemingly built-in talent for understatement. A butler let them in, and Jerry was startled by the hectic activity inside. In one room on their left, telexes and leased wires ticked and tapped out their messages. In another room, on the right, several computer technicians were busy feeding information to busily working computers. Several people moved by briskly, carrying slips of paper to be coordinated or processed into the information-gathering machines.

The man moving toward them down the long corridor was plump, neat, and looked as though he never perspired. "Mr. Questor?" he said. "I am Forbes. Coordinator."

"Very good," Questor said. He waved a hand to indicate Jerry to Forbes. "This is Jerry Robinson. Results?"

Forbes rumpled his forehead slightly and shrugged. "Negative on Vaslovik. Your holdings are . . . doing very well." He shot a look at Jerry, as though afraid to reveal too much in front of him.

"Mr. Robinson is my friend, Forbes. You may say to him anything you would say to me."

127

"Yes, sir. This way, please, gentlemen."

Forbes led the way down the corridor to a large, sunlit room decorated in soft tones of beige and brown and brightened with touches of orange and yellow. It had been set up as an office—clearly Questor's. The furniture was efficient and spartan, minimally designed for comfort. Once again, Jerry wondered at Lady Helena's ability to get exactly the right things done whenever necessary. He sat down on one of the couches while Questor sat down at the desk and quickly scanned through several reports left there for him.

The door opened, and a stately, black-haired woman entered. She was perhaps forty, but her face was unlined, and the grace of her movements suggested a far younger woman. She carried another report, which she held out to Questor.

"Mrs. Eleanor Chavez, sir. Formerly chief of research for Security Council," Forbes said.

Questor extended his hand to shake hers, rather than to take the report. "I have heard of you, Mrs. Chavez. If you can give me the details of what you have found . . . just in summary . . ."

She recited the facts in a lightly accented voice that made English sing. Jerry noticed Questor look up at her sharply as she began to speak, and he had a distinct impression that the android actually *enjoyed* simply listening to the sound of her voice.

"Vaslovik, Emile . . . date and place of birth unknown. Doctorate of physics, the Sorbonne, 1923 . . . parenthetically, middle-aged at the time. Academic posts: full professor Nuremberg, 1926–29. Sorbonne, 1929–37. University of Ankara, Columbia . . . the dates are—"

"The dates are known," Questor interrupted gently. "I prefer information prior to his matriculation."

"Unobtainable, sir."

Questor paused for a moment, digesting that fact. "I see. Continue your work, please, Mrs. Chavez."

She left quickly, and Questor leafed through the rest of the reports on the desk. "Holdings report?" Forbes pressed one of the buttons on the desktop, and Questor nodded, having cataloged its location. He glanced over at Jerry. "This push-button world. It seems appropriate, does it not, Jerry?"

Jerry grinned and ducked his head to hide a chuckle. Forbes did not understand the joke, and he was too polite to inquire. The door opened again, and a middle-aged, scholarly-looking man entered, also carrying a sheaf of accounting reports.

"Isaac Schoenberg," Forbes said. "Formerly securities analyst, Swiss Credit, Geneva."

"Mr. Schoenberg," Questor said. "By now you should have adequate information from Mr. Campbell in London as to the standings of the various investments he has made on my order."

"I . . . I hardly know where to start. This is so remarkable."

Questor held out his hand for the accounts. "May I, please?"

As Questor scanned them briefly, Schoenberg lifted his shoulders in a confused shrug. "I do not know how it was accomplished, but you . . . have nothing to worry about."

Jerry rose and came to Questor's side to look over his shoulder at the accounting sheets. His eyes opened wide, and he involuntarily caught his breath. "I'll say! Questor, from that . . . ah . . . original investment?"

"Yes. I regret concentrating so much at one time, but it is necessary."

"I haven't anything against a few dozen million dollars —but why, Questor?"

Questor looked up at him, tilting his head slightly to the right in his quizzical manner. "You have forgotten, Jerry. I have but three days left. The imperative is stronger."

Jerry straightened; he *had* forgotten. Silently he turned away from Questor and went back to sit on the couch. Questor went about his business, leaving Jerry to slump miserably in the corner. Questor gave further instructions to Schoenberg, and Jerry reflected on whether he would have been so open about them if he'd known that this entire place was bugged. He glanced around the room, though he knew the bugs would have been planted so not even the best investigators could find them. Darro would have seen to that. Jerry felt his stomach start to knot in pain. To take his mind off the ache, he concentrated on what Questor was saying to Forbes.

"Every conceivable effort must be made to trace the life of Vaslovik back to the day he was born. Where? When? Who were his parents? I find it inconceivable that such information, regarding one of the greatest humans of the age, is unobtainable. And you will continue the search for that ship, or boat."

"Yes, sir. Immediately," Forbes said.

Jerry paced irritably, taking in the sophisticated recording equipment, the "rifle bug" that could be aimed out the window and bring in a conversation across the street. In fact, this room *was* directly across the street from the townhouse. Several tape recorders decorated the table near the window. One spun slowly, playing back Questor's distinctive voice.

" . . I find it almost inconceivable that such information, regarding one of the greatest humans of the age, is unobtainable. And you will continue the search for that ship, or boat."

Darro flicked off the tape recorder. "They haven't found it yet . . . nor Vaslovik."

"You don't need me to tell you that. With all this slick junk of yours, you hear every word that goes on in that house."

Darro turned up the corners of his mouth. "Indeed I do. And I have heard a few things our scientist friends from the project would give an arm and a leg to know."

"I'll bet," Jerry snapped. He swung around on Darro. "How'd you get them off our backs, anyway?"

"I told them I arranged Questor's escape—that I, and I alone, would know where he is at all times—and if he was interfered with, I would destroy him."

"Well, in a few days it becomes an academic question, doesn't it?"

Darro lifted his hands in a helpless gesture, something that did not happen often with him. "Vaslovik's machine. The funny thing is, Questor is not the mystery. Vaslovik is. I have had placed at my disposal the full informational and intelligence sources of the United States, Great Britain, France, the Soviet Union, and China . . . and can't find out a damned thing about this Vaslovik! The most brilliant scientist of our times—but as far as I can find out, he was never even born!"

Jerry looked up, confused, groping for words. "But that can't be. I mean—Einstein, Planck, Galileo, Leeuwenhoek—the basic facts of their lives are known. Surely—"

"Nothing!" Darro exploded. "Not a damned word. Not a fact. Not a birth record . . . a death record . . . no passport, no naturalization certificate. Nothing!"

"That's impossible. No one exists in this world without papers—not in Vaslovik's kind of world, anyway."

"Yes. That's impossible," Darro said. He stared at Jerry grimly. "But it's true."

Questor found Jerry in the sitting room, buried in the depths of a massive chair. A bottle and some glasses stood next to him on a side table, but they were untouched. Jerry sat unmoving, his head in his hands, shrouded in misery.

"Jerry?" Questor said quietly. He frowned as Jerry lifted his head to reveal his drawn, haggard face. "It disturbs me to see you like this."

"Two days, Questor. Just two more days."

"I have selected an area in the mid-Sahara for the detonation. I had thought of the Marianas Trench, but damage to aquatic life would be—"

Jerry jumped to his feet, angry, shouting, "Is that all that's worrying you? Finding a place where you can blow up without hurting anything?"

"It seems to me a matter of valid concern," Questor said gently.

"You're going to die. Don't you understand that?"

Questor shook his head and said softly, "Jerry, we

have spoken of this before. It will be nothing more than
a machine performing another programmed function."

"That's a lie!" Tears suddenly running down his cheeks,
Jerry grabbed Questor by the shoulders and tried to shake
him violently. Of course, Questor did not shake—but
Jerry did. "Don't you understand? You're a human being!"

Questor took Jerry's hands and held them still. "You
will harm yourself, my friend. You built me well." Jerry
started to interrupt, but Questor continued. "I am not a
human being, Jerry. I am a machine. I think, yes, and
therefore I am. But *what* am I? I do not know the answer. I feel I never shall."

"Then the ship," Jerry said desperately. "The ship is
the answer. The *Golden Hind?* The *Queen Mary?* The
Nautilus? The *Constitution?* The *Nina* or the *Pinta* or the
Santa Maria? Questor, in the name of God . . ."

Questor stared at him, and Jerry stopped. For a moment there seemed to be a light of recognition in Questor's
eyes. Then it failed. "I thought . . ." Questor began, then
he let the thought trail away. He turned and walked from
the room, leaving Jerry to stare dully after him.

Darro was engaged in conversation on a special red
phone. Jerry sat across from him, nursing what he expected was the beginning of an ulcer. It gave him only
mild satisfaction to hear Darro's end of the conversation
and to imagine the other side of it.

"Dr. Gorlov, you already know all I intend to tell you
at this time. And you already know it will do you no
good to try to trace this call or locate me by triangulation.
I've taken care of that. In short, replay this message to
your . . . friends . . . and remember it yourself. Don't call
me. I'll call you." He slammed down the phone. "Idiots!
Suspicious, hostile, power-grabbing—"

"What's the difference?" Jerry interrupted. "Twenty-
eight hours isn't enough for them to do any damage."

Darro tapped his fingers on the phone, then took a
deep breath and leaned forward to rub his fatigue-red-
dened eyes. "I've already made arrangements to clear the
area he selected in the Sahara. He was right. The wind

currents are perfect. Fallout will be highly restricted. The
only danger might be to wandering tribes who entered
the area by mistake."

Jerry stood up, angrily. "What the hell are you, the
Atomic Energy Commission? You're talking about the
death of my friend!"

Darro looked at him dubiously. "Your *friend* is a practical man, and so am—" He paused, realizing something.
"I called him a man, didn't I?"

"He is," Jerry said quietly. "The best one I know."

Jerry returned to the townhouse slumped, weary, de-
spairing. Forbes came to the door to let him in when he
rang. "Where is he?" Jerry asked.

Forbes answered immediately, without hesitation. There
was really only one "he" in the townhouse. "Mr. Questor
went out."

"Out?"

"I believe he said something about the park, Mr. Robinson."

"Central Park?"

Forbes shrugged helplessly. "He seems to have a peculiar liking for the place, sir. He's gone there several times
in the past few days."

Jerry didn't stop to hear the rest of it. He turned and
ran down the steps to wave the always-waiting limousine
up to the curb. He hopped in and directed the chauffeur
to Central Park.

He found Questor tossing crumbs to a flock of cooing
pigeons who fought for the bread morsels with an invading
band of sparrows. Questor looked around as Jerry
pounded up to him and skidded to a halt on the slick
grass.

"Questor, it isn't safe here. They could find you."

"No." The statement was so flat, no argument could
be mounted against it. Questor clearly saw no way anyone
could harm him now. He gestured toward the squabbling
flock of birds, and he shook his head sadly. "They always

seem so hungry, shouldering one another out of the way even though there is enough for all."

Jerry's voice shook, and he tried to control it—but failed. "It's . . . Questor, it's time to go."

Questor nodded slowly, reluctant to leave. He looked around, taking in the friendly trees and shrubs and the far-off laughter of playing children. Suddenly he froze, staring at the play area.

"Questor, what is it?"

Questor raised a hand to gesture him silent. The children were climbing all over a sturdy reproduction of Noah's Ark. It was a dozen feet long, ten feet high, with wooden animals dutifully marching up the ramp. Suddenly Questor saw the missing pieces of the puzzle fall into place.

"A boat from a legend, Jerry." He turned back to Jerry with an expression that could be called excited. "Vaslovik! I know his location now." He hurried toward the limousine, with Jerry running after him.

"It's halfway around the world, Questor!"

Questor slid into the limousine, half pulling Jerry after him. "All the more reason to hurry, my friend."

16

A radio beeper with a directional device sat before Darro, softly emitting its steady, pinging signal. Darro swayed slightly as his car took a sharp corner, racing for the airport. Fortunately, he had been able to have Questor's limousine bugged as well as the townhouse. Therefore he had been able to pick up Questor's instructions to have the private jet standing by at Kennedy International and he learned that Questor and Robinson were leaving immediately. Their destination had not yet been determined. Neither had mentioned it aloud. Darro had called ahead to have a radar jet with Air Force personnel waiting for him. He began to have a ridiculous feeling that he was playing tag with a mischievous child. But he knew time *was* running out for Questor; he had no doubt of that fact. If Vaslovik—and the answer to the puzzle—could be found before that, only Questor could do it.

Jerry was strapped in the right-hand seat, with his eyes screwed shut, when Questor got his takeoff clearance from the flight controller in the tower and began taxiing down the runway. The jet lifted off and surged upward. Jerry opened one eye and risked a peek out the window. They had not only made it, they were apparently having no problems at all. He looked across at Questor, who sat easily in the left-hand seat, piloting the plane.

Questor caught the look and managed a reassuring smile at Jerry. It was one of the few times he had even tried to smile, and it worked surprisingly well. "You see, my friend? What can better understand a machine than

135

another machine?" He reached cruising altitude and put the jet on automatic pilot. "You have the maps?"

Jerry nodded and spread out detail maps of Turkey, Iran, and Soviet border areas. He studied one in particular for a moment, then pinpointed a spot with his finger. "Here it is—an abandoned emergency wartime strip at approximately latitude forty-four degrees twenty seconds, longitude forty degrees fifteen seconds."

Questor glanced at the map, taking it in with one look, then nodded. He had the position in his computer banks and would not need the map again. "Lady Helena has arranged a land vehicle as requested?"

"A fully gassed, four-wheel-drive jeep will be waiting for us at the airstrip." He studied the map again and tapped the point they had decided upon. "Are you certain this is it?"

"Mount Ararat, where legend says the Ark of Noah came to rest."

"And Vaslovik is on that mountain?"

Questor nodded, absolutely certain. "He is there—somewhere. And if I don't find him in time"—he looked at Jerry and enunciated the last words a bit too clearly—"that mountain will become a molehill."

Jerry tilted his head slightly to the right in unconscious imitation of Questor's habit. "What?"

"It was meant to be humorous," Questor said earnestly.

Jerry stared at him; and a grin spread across his mouth, crinkling up the corners of his eyes as it stretched. "I don't think automation is going to worry the Comedians' Guild."

The larger Air Force jet that carried Darro remained a carefully discreet distance behind the private plane Questor flew. An Air Force colonel was bent over a map beside Darro, tracing out a projected course. "Bearing due east exactly. Following along that line—Azores, Lisbon, Rome, Athens, Ankara."

"And?" Darro asked.

The colonel shrugged. "That's all we can project from this point. We can get more as we move further east."

"What's the standing on surveillance?"

"His plane will be under constant radar surveillance. French stations will pick it up over the mid-Atlantic, then we'll catch it again. British and Russian stations at the same time. The Chinese will just have to take our word for it."

"Don't bet on it," Darro snapped. "Repeat to all concerned my earlier message. Under no circumstances is that plane to be interfered with. Wherever it wants to land, let it land—and let it take off again."

"Yes, sir," the colonel said. "Sir, may I ask . . . why not just grab him?"

Darro looked up at him with cold, veiled eyes. "Do you hunt, Colonel?" The officer shook his head. "Well, you should still know you need a hunting dog to flush a bird. In this case, the bird has been reluctant to show his face for three years. Now we have the hunter to make him break cover."

"Uh . . . yes, sir. If you'll excuse me?"

Darro nodded, and the officer left to confer with the pilot. Darro knew his explanation hadn't really explained anything, but there wasn't any easy way to tell someone that the man you were following was a walking bomb. *Man.* Darro frowned in annoyance as he realized that he had been referring to Questor as a human again. *Damn Robinson!* The young engineer's insistence on Questor's "humanity" was starting to get to him, too. Darro let his eyes wander to the steadily ticking beeper device. It reassured him. No *man* would have a radio transmitter sealed deep inside him.

Questor's eyes routinely scanned the radarscope and noted the blips coming in from three directions. He turned to Jerry and tapped the screen of the scope. "We are being followed by aircraft directly behind us, and smaller clusters of aircraft to the right. Darro, I presume."

Jerry suppressed his surprise and shrugged. "I presume. Of course, it could be just routine air traffic."

"I think not, Jerry. It is most unusual for a private jet to be escorted by squadrons of Mysteres and Phantoms."

"You're right," Jerry said reluctantly. "Darro could call out that kind of show."

"Yes," Questor said. "A capable, ingenious man. And so are you, my friend."

Jerry snapped a look at him, startled. And he wished Questor had said anything in the world but that.

Questor put the plane down for refueling in Lisbon and took off again as soon as the ship was gassed. As Darro had instructed, Questor's requests were carried out immediately and no one interfered with him. Jerry managed to sleep all the way to Athens, where Questor again landed to top off the fuel tanks. The android was as quiet as possible, but Jerry woke when the plane's engines whined up to top power for takeoff. He stretched and straightened in the co-pilot's seat and rubbed the sleep from his eyes.

"You get any rest?" he asked sleepily.

Questor concentrated on the takeoff until he was safely out of the traffic pattern and pushing the jet up to specified altitude. "Jerry," he said, "even if I required rest, which you know I do not, I could not stop now."

Jerry let him fly silently for a moment, then he asked, "How much more time?"

"Four hours, fifteen minutes, twenty-one seconds," Questor replied automatically.

The private jet landed at the abandoned airstrip three hours later. It wasn't the smoothest landing Jerry had ever been through. The old runway had been strictly an emergency landing site to begin with, and it hadn't been touched for thirty years. As the jet bounced over the rough ground, Jerry could see the jeep waiting, unattended, near the end of the landing strip. Questor cut the engines. The two men then climbed down out of the plane and ran to the jeep.

Questor reached it first, and had it started and into first gear when Jerry jumped in beside him. The android shifted gears rapidly and headed the vehicle down a winding path that had no business calling itself a road. A mountain range thrust up toward the sky in the near distance. Lady Helena's scouts had already been over the path and assured them, through her, that the jeep could navigate all the way to the foot of the mountain.

A jet soared overhead, skimming low. Jerry pulled out a pair of field glasses and managed to hold them to his eyes despite the jouncing and swaying of the jeep. The big plane settled toward the earth and angled in for a landing at the emergency airstrip.

"Darro," Jerry said.

Questor merely nodded and continued to maneuver the vehicle over the ruts and stones toward Mount Ararat. Jerry put the binoculars up to his eyes again to scan a rising cloud of dust on the horizon line. He could not make it out at that distance, especially fighting the tilt and jolt of the jeep; but that much dust could mean only one thing . . . a vehicle column heading in their direction. Probably troop carriers and weapons trucks.

Jerry had guessed correctly. As Darro's plane touched down and rolled to a halt, the first of the columns had reached the landing strip. A jeep-load of officers wheeled up as Darro climbed down out of the big jet. One of them, an American Army colonel named Hendricks, jumped out to join Darro.

"Which way are they headed?" Darro asked sharply.

"Roughly toward Mount Ararat, sir."

They had reached the side of the jeep, and Darro stopped, staring strangely at Hendricks for a second. *Boats. That frantic search for boats. That was what it meant—the key to the location of—what? Vaslovik? Something else?* Darro shoved the jeep driver out of the way and took the wheel himself. The other officers cleared out at a motion from Hendricks, but the colonel chose to jump in beside Darro as he gunned the jeep toward the mountain.

The road had stopped, petering out to a goat path and then disappearing altogether. Questor had merely shifted down and kept on, skillfully taking the jeep over rough, seesawing terrain that climbed higher into the foothills of the fabled mountain. Jerry anxiously glanced at his watch. "Half an hour left."

Questor, intent upon his driving, stared straight ahead. "Twenty-nine minutes, thirty-one seconds," he corrected mechanically.

Jerry nodded. Questor was right, of course. Suddenly the android braked the jeep to a stop and turned to him. "Get out now, my friend. There is rock shelter here in case I fail."

Jerry was still, staring stubbornly back at him. "I'm not leaving."

Questor hesitated, debated arguing with him. But the solid core of determination that made Jerry both valuable and vulnerable would not be shaken. Questor could see that in the straight set of Jerry's mouth and the unblinking look of his eyes. He put the jeep into gear again and started forward, quickly accelerating.

Finally, they reached a point beyond which the jeep could not climb. There were too many rocks and steep inclines. A tumbled-down shepherd's hut stood nearby, abandoned long ago. Questor paused to look around. The area was somehow vaguely familiar to him—he did not know how or why. Jerry nervously looked at his watch again.

"Fourteen minutes."

Questor turned to him, pleading. "Jerry, you gave me life. I have no wish to cause your death."

"Then stop talking." Jerry turned and scrambled out of the jeep, running uphill. Questor followed, easily catching up, and then pacing his friend.

"It will not be much further," Questor said.

Jerry puffed and slipped and struggled over the rocks behind him. "How . . . how do you . . . know?"

"I feel it." Questor was too far in the lead to see Jerry's surprised look.

Darro raced his jeep up and stopped beside the one Questor and Robinson had abandoned. He cut the engine and turned on Hendricks. "Don't ask me any questions. In exactly"—he checked his watch—"ten minutes and twelve seconds, a bomb is probably going to go off up there. Keep all troops at least twenty miles from this point."

"You're going up there?"

"I wouldn't miss it for the world, Colonel." Darro grabbed a pair of binoculars, jumped out of the jeep, and started to run up the slope. Hendricks got on the radio and transmitted the message. Then he whirled the jeep around and headed back down the slope as fast as he could.

Questor and Jerry burst out into a natural amphitheater curved into the side of the slope. Above them rose a sheer rock wall. In the center of the bowl-like space was a huge stone monolith, a sort of crude column, resting on a flat boulder. It stood like a solitary temple pillar—immeasurably ancient—and somehow, not quite of this earth.

Questor stopped, closed his eyes, and waited, as motionless as the stones around them. "Yes," he said softly. "Yes." His eyes snapped open and he went immediately to the great monolith. His arms went around it, and he began to twist it counterclockwise. It took every ounce of his great strength, but the rock began to move—and to *click,* as if it were some giant combination lock. Jerry stared in silence, too awed to speak. Questor slowly moved the boulder around until it locked in place. Then he straightened and stared up at the rugged face of the cliff just above them.

An area of the mountainside a dozen feet in diameter began to shimmer, to quiver. Then, with a hollow rushing sound, the glittering area *disappeared,* revealing a long, glassine tunnel which led deep into the heart of the mountain.

"Come! I have less than one minute," Questor said. He ran forward, and Jerry obediently followed. They had no sooner stepped through the mountainside opening and into the tunnel than the area shimmered again and became instantly solid. They were sealed in.

Darro had arrived, scrambling among the rocks, in time to see Questor move the giant boulder and to watch the tunnel entrance appear. He saw it close after them again with that unearthly quivering gleam, and he chose not to question it, but to accept it. He ran forward, toward the monolith "lock."

17

The tunnel stretched on and on, glinting and winking from light sources Jerry's human eyes could not detect. The floor was absolutely smooth, and Jerry had a hard time keeping his balance and trying to make speed. Questor put on a burst of speed and left Jerry far behind. Jerry slipped and fell; and by the time he had regained his feet, Questor had vanished. Jerry ran a few steps, slowed to look at the luminous dial of his watch, and cried out in a scream of desolate despair.

"Questor—it's too late!"

Outside, in the natural amphitheater, Darro paused to glance at his watch. He threw himself down behind the monolith instinctively, not stopping to realize it would not matter. *Now!*

Nothing happened.

Slowly he got to his knees and then up to his feet. He checked his watch again. It was accurate to the split second—and it was past the time the android was due to explode. Darro knew enough about Vaslovik to know that the android would have detonated as scheduled—unless something in that tunnel stopped it. He flung himself at the monolith, but it resisted his human effort. Desperately he searched for something to help—a lever—and he found one in the sturdy branch of a tree lying among the rocks. He began to pry at the monolith's base.

Jerry had braced himself for the explosion, knowing that in this confined space it would hit too fast for him to ever feel it. When nothing happened, he cautiously moved

143

ahead and saw the tunnel widening into a great natural chamber in the heart of the mountain. As he stepped into it, he froze, struck with awe at the sight of what the chamber contained.

The scene was otherworldly. Huge, shimmering, transparent, extradimensional devices rimmed the room. Some hardly seemed to be there at all, as though they were partly in this world and partly in another. The entire hall-like chamber was vaulted with some chimeralike glimmer, shot through with shifting red, blue, and violet light patterns which seemed suspended, half real, in mid-air. As in the tunnel, the whole chamber was diffused with glowing light from unseen sources. One wall was blank. But it was so indistinct, so hard to place in space and time as he knew it, that Jerry was not sure it was a wall at all. It was directly across the chamber from the tunnel entrance where Jerry stood.

And Questor. Questor stood in the center of the chamber, in the strongest pattern of mid-air light points, lifting his hands, controlling their number, their hues, as if operating extradimensional devices from another world. His eyes were closed, and a play of the constantly changing light patterns moved up and down over his body. In some dark and frightened corner of his mind, Jerry recognized this incredible nonlinear, nonmatter equipment as a laboratory of a hundred thousand years from now, the technical playthings of a race which might well have outgrown technology.

He studied his friend. Questor now stood unmoving in the play of unreal light. There was a humming, a disturbing sound; and Jerry realized that it was all being directed at Questor. *What was it doing to him?*

The glowing and the strange humming suddenly stopped, and the light patterns around Questor faded away completely. They left a new Questor—one totally assured, totally aware of his purpose, of what he was, and why. He stared at Jerry for a moment—and from those eyes, which previously were without expression, there came a new look of compassion and wisdom. He smiled at his friend.

Then a deep, familiar voice boomed hollowly into the chamber. "Questor?"

Questor turned. "I am here, Vaslovik."

The far wall, the blank wall with no equipment in front of it, shimmered the same way the hillside had shimmered. Then it faded and vanished. Jerry caught his breath and stepped back slightly from the shock of what he saw.

Closest to the chamber was a large, empty slab. Next to it was another, and beyond that, others—many others, fading back into a shadowy infinity. On the second slab lay a man wearing a business suit. Jerry recognized him as his mentor, Emil Vaslovik. The scientist lay on the slab without moving, but his open eyes stared unwinkingly at the ceiling. Each of the slabs beyond him, stretching backward into the distance, held the body of another man, though the costumes were vastly different. Next to Vaslovik, there was a man in a frock coat and a beard from the mid-eighteenth century. Beyond him lay a rather regally clad figure from the sixteenth century, apparently lifeless, but perfectly whole. Other bodies ranged back beyond his, the costumes going back to the most primitive, gaudy finery of early priests and kings. Who knew who these men might have been? Charlemagne might lie there, Galileo, Leonardo, Alexander the Great, Socrates, Plato, Plutarch. Ranks upon ranks of them were there, moving backward in space and, somehow, Jerry knew, in time.

Questor moved forward, and Jerry followed him, frightened, but unable to stop after coming this far. They stopped at the foot of Vaslovik's slab. Questor paused for a moment, studying his creator. Vaslovik was of average height, his hair a fading white and his blue eyes gradually losing the brightness of life. Deep lines were etched in his face, the imprint of care. His features were intelligent, compassionate, telling a tale of a life spent in learning and giving. Vaslovik's lips moved slightly, and Questor stepped forward so that his creator could see him.

"You have received the Truth?" Vaslovik asked. Though his mouth made little movement, his voice boomed out, amplified.

"I have received it," Questor said quietly. He looked up, beyond Vaslovik, to the line of slabs reaching out to an infinite past. "Since the dawn of this world—since our Masters left the first of us here—we have served this species, Man."

Jerry twitched, startled. *We* have served . . . *our* Masters . . . what was Questor saying? His eyes darted from Questor to Vaslovik and back. Had the equipment here driven him mad, loosened the practical and logical computer mind from its moorings? Then Vaslovik spoke, and Jerry knew.

"Each of us, at the end of his time, has assembled his own replacement. But man's quantum advance in physics found me unprepared. The new radiations affected the plasma in my brain case. Your design corrects this fault. You will function your full span, as planned."

"Not entirely as planned, brother. Your activation tape was tampered with. Your location, other parts of it, were erased."

Vaslovik's eyes shifted to the young figure bending over him. "But you have arrived in time." A statement that was a question.

Questor hesitated, caught for a moment by an inexplicable inability to express the failure in himself. Then he said slowly and softly, "I am incomplete, Vaslovik. I cannot . . . feel. I am incapable of feeling the emotion which you and humans experience."

Vaslovik lay still, not even the shallow rise and fall of his chest moving, for almost sixty seconds. Then he resumed the breathing pattern that had halted to allow him to consult some inner voice. "You say you cannot feel emotion. Then you must be guided in this by a human."

Questor looked back at Jerry and nodded. "I select the man you chose to build me, my brother."

"No, that choice must be his." Vaslovik's voice had begun to fade, and his eyes dimmed. "Hear the laws, my brother. We protect, but we do not interfere. Man must make his own way. We guide him, serve him, aid him. But always without his knowledge."

"I hear and obey," Questor said.

Vaslovik appeared to be growing weaker much more rapidly . . . while Questor seemed to grow in strength. The older one moved his eyes slightly, refocusing on Jerry. "Jerry Robinson . . ."

Jerry stepped closer to the slab. He had worked for this man . . . he thought he knew him. The thoughts and fears he had entertained in the past week melted away, replaced by the respect he had always felt for Vaslovik. He was a good man; knowing he was an android couldn't change Jerry's feelings toward him, no matter how contradictory the idea seemed.

"In two hundred millennia, you are the only human creature who has joined us here in our truth. As mankind needs us, now we need one of you," Vaslovik said.

"I understand the responsibility."

"That which is on earth. Teach him error . . . weakness . . . compassion . . . empathy. You must give him those things of humanity he did not receive." Vaslovik's voice had grown so weak that it was almost a whisper. "I chose you with great care. I see now I have chosen correctly."

Jerry touched Vaslovik's hand as a promise and a seal. "I'll do my best, sir."

Vaslovik's dimming eyes moved to Questor's face pleadingly. "For three years . . . I have lain here . . . only my mind functioning . . . and I am weary. Let me pass now, brother."

Questor stepped close to Vaslovik and carefully inserted his right hand under the skull of his predecessor. "Pass on, brother," Questor said in benediction. His fingers moved. Vaslovik's eyes closed, and the faint lift of his chest held for a moment, then fell with a soft sigh. He was still and at peace at last. Jerry stared at him for a long moment, awed and moved.

Without looking around, Questor spoke. "Please come in, Mr. Darro."

Jerry whipped around to see Darro standing at the tunnel entrance to the chamber. He did not know how long Darro had been there, nor even how he had managed to find the entry to the tunnel. But he realized, as Darro came closer, that the man who lived his life as a cynic was shaken and even a trifle hesitant.

Darro stopped a few feet from them and looked around the chamber at the row of slabs and finally at Questor. "Well, I've spent half my life wondering how we got this far without killing each other off. Now I know, I'm still not sure I like it."

Questor shook his head, in pity . . . a special kind of pity reserved for ones like Darro. "You heard, but you did not understand. At certain pivotal moments—some so seemingly trivial as to escape notice—we assist men in altering the course of events. We *assist*, Mr. Darro. Perhaps only one word in the right ear, a child protected so he will grow into a man who will be needed—but Man always makes his own destiny."

"There is only one empty slab left, Questor," Darro said.

"There is no need for more. My span is two hundred years. If the race of Man outlives me, it will have seen the end of its childhood."

"Except Man will never make it, Questor," Darro said bitterly. He flung out an arm, pointing at the tunnel. "They're waiting for you out there. They'll take you apart rather than let you go free." He met Questor's eyes directly in a level stare. "I would have. I can't see why these 'Masters' of yours even bothered with us."

"It has never been what Man *is*," Questor said softly, "but what he has the potential of becoming."

Jerry straightened up suddenly, guiltily. He had almost forgotten the deal he had made with Darro. "Maybe Man's too rotten to make it, Questor. When I tell you what I planted on you—"

"I know, Jerry," Questor interrupted. He reached into his pocket and brought out the small directional transmitter. "I stopped its transmission when we landed here."

"You knew?" Jerry said incredulously. "Questor, you *knew* I put that in you and you didn't do anything about it?"

Questor tilted his head slightly to the right, studying

Jerry quizzically. "Of course, I am programmed to know if an alien object is placed in me. As for not removing it, such an action would have informed Mr. Darro that I was aware of the transmitter and he would have stopped us before we arrived here."

"But you didn't know we'd find Vaslovik before your time was up," Jerry said.

"In that case, the transmitter would have meant nothing anyway."

Darro suddenly held out his hand. "Give it to me."

Questor stared at him for a long moment, gauging him, weighing the implications of what he'd said. "Are you certain, Mr. Darro?"

"The first time I've ever been this certain of anything in this world," Darro said firmly.

"You doubted the worthiness of your race. Have you not just proved it?"

Darro smiled a genuine smile, not the faint crook of the corners of the mouth. But it was grim, and Jerry realized that the hard-bitten cynic had returned.

"Maybe I just don't like being taken care of," Darro said. He held out his hand again, and this time Questor put the small transmitter into Darro's palm. Darro turned and ran for the tunnel entrance. In a moment, he was gone from view.

Jerry turned to Questor, not quite sure of what had just taken place. Questor returned Jerry's stare with level steadiness. "We will wait ten minutes. Then it will be safe to leave."

"You can't be sure of that."

"Yes, I can," Questor said. "Mr. Darro has guaranteed it. And I believe you once said his word was comparable to precious metal."

"Good as gold."

"Yes."

"Questor, how can you trust him when you know how he tracked you down?"

Questor smiled sadly and glanced around at the long row of occupied slabs. "He is a man, Jerry. The collective memory now ingrained in me tells me there have been many like him before. He doubts the good in Man; he wonders why your race was brought forth and why it survives. Yet he carries in himself many of the virtues that helped Man survive—honor, courage, a refusal to *stop* surviving no matter what the future. He will not fail us."

The tunnel "sensed" Darro's presence and automatically opened with a roaring rush of sound. Darro stepped out and very deliberately rolled down the rocky slope to the natural amphitheater. When he picked himself up, he noted that he had managed to get several bruises, a cut over one eye—giving him a thoroughly battered look. It should do, he thought to himself. Then he began to make his way down the side of the mountain.

He reached the jeep Questor and Robinson had abandoned, and climbed into it. Questor had left the keys in the ignition, and Darro gunned the engine to life, wheeled the jeep around, and headed for the lower slopes, where the troops should be waiting.

Jerry and Questor emerged from the tunnel five minutes later. They picked their way down toward the amphitheater, where the huge monolith reigned. Jerry heard the swirling rush of air behind them and looked back to watch the tunnel close. It shimmered and swirled and finally faded into what appeared to be a perfectly ordinary cliff face.

Questor had paused beside the large boulder "lock" that opened the tunnel entrance. As Jerry came up beside him, Questor motioned at the tree branch Darro had left jammed under the flat boulder after he had forced the stones around and into the tunnel-opening position. "He must have used this as a lever to pry the lock," Questor said.

Jerry studied it and agreed. Then he looked at the tree branch and the stones, and then around at the terrain. "Questor, where did he get the tree branch?" He waved his hand around to indicate. "It's just rocks and dirt. No trees, Questor. No trees except for some young ones down closer to the lower slopes. So how did that very handy tree branch get up here for him to use as a lever?"

"I do not know, Jerry. Perhaps it was the work of *your* creator."

Darro drove the jeep crazily, weaving from side to side, almost tipping as he hit a deep rut, and jounced to a spine-jolting halt near Colonel Hendricks' vehicle. As the officer ran toward him, Darro stumbled from the jeep and slumped against it, seemingly exhausted and shaken. More than that, he seemed frightened.

"What happened?" Hendricks yelled.

Darro's voice shook uncertainly. "Vaslovik . . . he *was* insane. He hid several small nuclear bombs up there! The android has them now!" He wiped away blood that had trickled down from a cut under his eye. It smeared into the dirt on his face, giving him a grotesque mask.

Hendricks stared at him, dumbfounded, for an instant. Then he found his voice. "Good Lord! *That thing could touch off a war!*"

"That's exactly what Vaslovik designed it for. Inform all units that we hid a transmitter device in the android's body—565 megacycles. I doubt if you can pick it up in these hills, but the minute you do hear it, send in the air units." He turned back to the jeep. "I'll inform the ground troops."

"Yes, sir." Hendricks ran toward the radio transmitter in his command jeep.

Darro climbed into Questor's vehicle and gunned it away, speeding rapidly back toward the airstrip. The small private jet Questor and Robinson had flown there rested on the tired, weathered runway like a sleek young bird in an old nest. Darro ironically wondered if he had learned to fly jets for just this moment. Had some android put the right word in someone's ear about *him?* He parked the jeep and hurried to the jet. As he climbed in and settled in the left hand seat, he briefly reflected on the question he had posed himself. *Had* he been manipulated all his life? Was he being manipulated now? He decided he was not. There never was a decision he had made without a clear and hard-eyed look at where it would lead him. He had made the same kind of decision back in the alien chamber.

He leaned forward and began to throw switches systematically. The jet engines whined to life. Then Darro brought the transmitting device from his pocket, set it down beside him, and threw the switch on it.

The young sergeant operating the triangulation station suddenly stiffened, listening intently to a sound in his earphones. He twisted around toward Colonel Hendricks, who stood by, waiting. "There it is, sir."

"Notify the air units," Hendricks barked over his shoulder. "We'll give them the coordinates in a minute."

Questor and Jerry waited in the silent amphitheater on the mountain, looking out toward the plain. Neither had spoken; they just waited. Questor was deeply thoughtful, as if he were scanning all the material in his computer banks to find an answer where there was none. Of course, he had done that before; but this time he had an answer. It was the *reason* that mystified him. Suddenly he lifted his head, hearing something with his hypersensitive ears that Jerry could not pick up.

"Questor?" Jerry said, noticing the android's alert, tense posture.

Questor waved a hand to still him. "A moment, Jerry. It will end soon."

Jerry scanned the sky, looking where Questor did, squinting into the bright clear blue over the plain. "I can't see anything."

"I wish I could not."

The private jet soared up, cutting the air with its slim body, then leveled off and ran for the sea. The sergeant at the triangulation station listened on his earphones intently, then looked toward Colonel Hendricks.

"Signal's airborne, sir. One of our squadrons and a French flight are pacing it."

Hendricks nodded curtly. "Tell them to shoot it down."

The private jet had a headstart, but there was no way it could outrun combat fighters. Two separate flights, French and American, wheeled in behind it. On a signal from their flight leaders, they fell into attack pattern with deadly precision.

Their prey climbed, clawing for altitude. The fighters mercilessly angled after it. One at a time, closely following one another, they released their missiles.

Jerry saw the last of it. No one could miss the giant ball of flame that erupted from high in that hard blue sky. Debris and smoke and fragments fell in black charred pieces to the ungiving earth. It was over, as Questor had promised. Jerry looked at him, shaken.

"I don't understand, Questor. If he hated humanity so much—"

Questor shook his head. "He hated what he believed Mankind is, Jerry. Not what it can become." He held out a hand, indicating a way down the slope in the direction opposite from the way they had come. "Come. We must leave here, in case they decide to search this area."

Jerry followed him down through the rocky terrain until they reached a footpath that wound toward the plain and the little farms in the distance. They walked silently for over an hour, each wrapped in a cocoon of his own thoughts. They had reached the outskirts of a small village before Jerry spoke.

"Where do you go now, Questor?"

"They know now that an android is possible, Jerry. And some may not believe I'm destroyed."

Jerry looked back toward the mountain. "You could always hide out in the chamber."

"I was not made to hide, nor was the chamber designed for that purpose. It is the beginning and the end for me and those who came before me. Until it is time for me to end, I must walk this world of yours and follow the imperative and the law given to me by Vaslovik." He stopped, reaching out to Jerry. "I need you to help me."

"With *your* mental and physical capabilities?"

"But I'm vulnerable, too, you saw that. I need assistance in other things . . . the illogical behavior pattern of the human species . . . social customs." He smiled wryly. "And trivial things, like humor." His smile faded, and his voice changed to a sad plea. "Vaslovik passed on too soon. Help me, Jerry. Please."

Jerry was bewildered and overwhelmed. "I don't know how I can, Questor. I'm . . . only human."

"That is why I need you. Remember, you heard the Truth in the chamber—and Vaslovik gave you a responsibility."

"He said I had a choice."

They stared at each other in silence until the spell was broken by a small girl who barreled around the corner of a house on her short little legs. She stopped, frozen by the sight of the two strangers. She was perhaps three, dressed in worn peasant clothing, her jet-black hair framing a piquant little face dominated by ebony eyes. She seemed to shrink away from them, frightened, curling in on herself away from these intruders. Her face crumpled up, preparatory to crying.

Questor turned toward Jerry, at a loss. "Jerry . . . a child. I have never—"

"It's easy. Smile at her. Laugh. Like this!" He knelt in the dust of the road, making himself eye level with the child, and smiled at her. She stared at him uncertainly. Jerry winked. Her little face began to smooth out and change to curiosity. Jerry glanced around and saw some delicate flowers growing wild in the grass beside him. He picked them and held them out to her, smiling. The child smiled back and stepped forward to take the flowers.

Jerry laughed, and the girl ran forward into his arms. He caught her and swung her high, up into his arms. Her happy giggle rang out, tickling the air. Jerry passed her over to Questor, who smiled at her. The girl flung her arms around Questor's neck and kissed his cheek. Jerry was sure he saw Questor's face turn a slightly deeper shade of pink. Questor put the girl up on his shoulder, holding her there as they walked through the village. The child squealed with delight and enjoyed the ride.

"You see," Questor said to Jerry, "I do need you. I would have made her cry." He glanced up at the small girl. "She is a feather. Her weight smiles on my shoulder. See how light humanity can be?"

Jerry looked at them both and finally nodded. "All right, Questor. I'll help where I can. At least you might need oiling now and then."

He grinned at Questor, and Questor smiled back. They had reached the edge of the village, and Questor put the child down. She hugged his neck again before she let him go and offered him one of the wild flowers. He took it and set it carefully in the buttonhole of his shirt. The girl turned to Jerry and gave him one of the delicate blossoms, too. Then she watched them as they walked away, down the dusty road. Once, Jerry looked back and saw her waving. He waved, and then turned away to follow Questor.

The scientists on Project Questor, the Army, and the Air Force greatly publicized the fact that the project had failed. The escaped lunatic the police had been hunting was reported captured. There was no public mention of an android.

But in London, Francis Scott Campbell invested and reinvested and placed the profits in a special Swiss account at the instructions he periodically received from a client. Lady Helena Trimble traveled and entertained and gathered information and always answered the phone, hoping to hear one certain voice. In New York, Forbes and Mrs. Chavez correlated information as requested by their employer. In a chamber deep in the heart of a mountain, an empty slab waited.

And on occasion, in various parts of the world, there were reports of a strangely formal, attractive blue-eyed man who came and went and did some things that changed lives, or prolonged some, or made the crops better, or averted a plague. He was always accompanied by a tall, rangy man with a warm, wide grin and twinkling eyes who had a magical knack for things mechanical.

The world went on its way as it always had—but somehow it seemed things were a little better than they had been before.